Are you ready to laugh?

"Lots of money in comedy," I say. "Lots of jobs."

"Like what?"

I think about it. "Comedian. Comic. Comic-book artist. Cartoonist. Comedy writer. Comedy club owner. Comedy club manager. Comedy club waiter. Clown. Court jester?"

"Court jester!"

"You never know when royalty may come back. Okay, comedy . . . you made me lose my train of thought . . . comedy . . . comedy . . . doctor. Comedy lawyer. Comedy plumber."

"Yeah, right," Dad mutters. "Or comedy Senator. Comedy President of the United States. There've been a lot of clowns in those jobs."

"See?" I say. "What did I tell you?"

OTHER BOOKS BY STEPHEN MANES

Chocolate-Covered Ants
Make Four Million Dollars by Next Thursday!
Be a Perfect Person in Just Three Days!
Chicken Trek
The Obnoxious Jerks
It's New! It's Improved! It's Terrible!
Some of the Adventures of Rhode Island Red
Monstra vs. Irving
The Great Gerbil Roundup
The Oscar J. Noodleman Television Network
That Game from Outer Space
Video War
Life Is No Fair!
The Hooples' Horrible Holiday
The Hooples' Haunted House
Slim Down Camp
Socko! Every Riddle Your Feet Will Ever Need
Pictures of Motion and Pictures that Move
The Boy Who Turned into a TV Set
I'll Live
Hooples on the Highway
Mule in the Mail
The Complete MCI Mail Handbook

WITH ESTHER MANES

The Bananas Move to the Ceiling

WITH PAUL ANDREWS

*Gates: How Microsoft's Mogul
Reinvented an Industry —
and Made Himself the Richest Man in America*

point

COMEDY HIGH

Stephen Manes

SCHOLASTIC INC.
New York Toronto London Auckland Sydney

No part of this publication may be reproduced in whole or in part, or stored in a retrieval system, or transmitted in any form or by any means, electronic, mechanical, photocopying, recording, or otherwise, without written permission of the publisher. For information regarding permission, write to Scholastic Inc., 555 Broadway, New York, NY 10012.

ISBN 0-590-44437-9

12 11 10 9 8 7 6 5 4 3 2 1   9   4 5 6 7 8 9/9

for Joanna

ONE

Kidnapped! Transported across the country! Forced into slavery! Roasted in my bed! Dragged kicking and screaming into an institution for the mentally deranged! Let's put it another way: A funny thing happened to me on the way to high school.

You know how it is. Things always sneak up when you're most relaxed, when you least expect them. In my case, it's summer, August, when I'm not even thinking about school. I'm home in Seattle, loafing around, watching the Mariners on TV. The Mariner left fielder dives for the ball, trying to turn a single into out number three. Instead he falls on his butt, turns the single into an inside-the-park home run, wipes out the Mariners' three-run lead. This kind of thing happens to the Mariners a lot.

1

So I am screaming some things I had better not repeat when my father comes through the door. The first words out of his mouth are "Son of mine," so I shut up. When Dad says, "Son of mine," something important is about to happen.

His next words are, "I've got good news and bad news."

There's only one kind of good news that would be important around here. "You found a new job?" I ask suspiciously.

Dad nods, grinning. "That's the good news."

"Congratulations!"

"Thanks."

I make a face. "What's the bad news?"

"The bad news is that the new job is in hell."

"Hell, Michigan?" I ask. There really is such a place. I learned this from a place mat.

He shakes his head. "Let me put it another way. The current temperature where we are going is 110 degrees. In the shade. And there is no shade."

I wince. In Seattle it almost never gets hot, even in summer. I hate hot weather. "Where is this hellhole? Death Valley?"

"Close. Death Valley's in California. We're going to Nevada."

I make a face. "Nevada? What's in Nevada besides sand?"

"Hoover Dam. Lake Mead." He opens his backpack and tosses a big Federal Express envelope at me. "The Valley of Fire State Park. Underground nuclear-test sites."

"Oh, great! Maybe we'll get lucky and be blown to smithereens!"

2

Dad ignores me. "Lake Tahoe. Reno. Las Vegas. Bright lights. Gambling. Tourism. The largest hotel in the free world."

"The toilet bowl of the free world is what this place sounds like." I rip open the envelope and take out a bunch of brochures.

Dad sticks his finger on one of them. "Here's where we're going."

"Carmody, Nevada?" I pronounce it "Car-MOE-dee."

"It's CAR-moe-dee," Dad corrects me. "Kind of like comedy with an R in the middle."

"So-o-o-o sorry," I reply.

"Boy, will I be happy when that phrase disappears from your vocabulary," Dad says. "So-o-o-o sorry," as you know, has been one of America's catchphrases ever since Harold Willsman, the green-faced comedian, got famous.

"So-o-o-o — "

"Yeah, I know," Dad says tolerantly. "So what do you think?"

I look at the brochure. At the top it says *Carmody, Nevada: We give Las Vegas a run for your money!* In the middle it says *All lucky! All fun! All hot! — It's Carmody!* At the bottom it says *Carmody, Nevada! Future Entertainment Capital of the World!* Well, it's the Exclamation Point Capital of the World, at least.

Behind the lettering is a picture of an enormous guy with a bright red nose and eighty-five chins and three stomachs and a string tie and a checkered coat so loud you can almost hear it barking. He is standing in front of this enormous theater sign that says **WELCOME TO CAR-**

MODY! in letters about as tall as he is.

I open the brochure. *Let us entertain you!* it exclaims on top. There are pictures of people gambling and swimming and shopping and bowling and dirt-biking, plus a bunch of hotels, a bunch of garish lighted signs, and a bunch of female dancers wearing a whole lot of feathers on their heads and not very many feathers or much of anything else on the rest of their bodies. Those are actually kind of interesting.

The back page has a map on it. This proves beyond a reasonable doubt that Carmody, Nevada, is in the absolute middle of nowhere — just across the river from Finger City, Arizona, a two-hour drive from Las Vegas, and God knows how far from anywhere else. "340 days of sun per year. Average temperature 87 degrees," I read out loud. "You weren't kidding about hell. You'd have to be nuts to move to this place."

Dad frowns. "Call us Cashew and Son."

I give him a dirty look and read on. "Three eighteen-hole golf courses. The International Museum of Snack Food Technology. And look at this: The airport is called the Carmody Interplanetary Spaceport."

"Noticed that," Dad says. "Apparently they want to attract tourists from Mars."

I smile a little. My father is known for his sarcasm. It's one of the reasons we move around so much. It's one of the reasons he named me Ivan when everybody thought it was important to hate Russians.

And it must be in our genes. I mean, I am a smartass. I have a big mouth. It has been known to get me in trouble. A friend of mine once said that if some villain abducted a whole bunch of people and said "One peep out of you and you're dead," I would probably be shot for saying "Peep." This friend was probably right.

I turn back to the brochure. "Population 7,432 happy, friendly folks," I read. "I wonder how many cranky, unfriendly folks they have."

Dad points a finger at me. "At least one, soon." He points at himself. "Maybe two."

The brochure says the town has elementary and middle schools, and the high school is supposed to open in September. "What do you know about this high school?" I ask suspiciously.

Dad shrugs. "Supposed to be quite a facility. They've got tons of tax money from gambling. And since it's new, you'll be starting even with everybody else."

"Right," I say. "Maybe I can take Snack Food Technology."

"You'd get an A in that for sure." Dad knows we ought to eat healthier stuff, but we are pizza and potato chip kinds of guys.

At the bottom of the page it says, "You'll love it so much, you'll want to stay for life!"

"Good slogan for a prison," I mutter.

"Well, your aunt moved there a couple of years ago. She seems to like it."

"Which aunt?"

"You know, my sister Penny? The one with a daughter about your age? They came to visit us in Pittsburgh?"

"Oh, right. Gilda! The one with the nose out to here. The one who hogged the bathroom the

5

whole time putting on her makeup."

"She's probably outgrown that."

"*That* nose had to outgrow her."

Dad gives me a dirty look. "Anyway, Penny's the one who found me the job."

"Which is what? Playing snack food theme songs?"

"Playing for a pit orchestra." My dad is a professional violist. Not violinist, though he can play the violin, too. But what he's really great at is the viola, and it's not like there are a million people out looking for viola players.

"Pit orchestra?" I ask. "You mean like the opera?"

Dad frowns. "Uh, not exactly."

"For what, then? A musical?"

Dad looks uncomfortable. "Sort of."

I suddenly get it. "One of *these* shows." I point to one of the women in nothing but feathers.

"It's not exactly Beethoven," Dad said. "In fact, it's crappy. But I've got to feed us, me lad."

"On what? Tarantulas? Cactus juice? This place definitely sounds sucko. Lame. The butt end."

"You'll probably get more use out of your telescope," Dad says.

"Well, whoopee-diddle," I sneer. I am sort of an amateur astronomer, and I have this really neat telescope my grandparents gave me, and it's true, in Seattle the skies are cloudy so often I don't get much chance to use it.

But hey, I love it here. We've been in this town almost two years now, and I have the greatest friends I've ever known. Even their parents are terrific. My dad is basically an indoor person, but my friends' parents are really into the outdoors. I've been skiing, sailing, hiking, biking, you name it. They take me so many places that at one point Dad actually asked me if I ever spent any time reading or doing my homework.

But for once in my life I keep my mouth shut. I don't rub it in. I know Dad likes it here, too, and he's looked all over for jobs. It just hasn't worked out. "Kidnapper," I say, sensing tears in the back of my eyes. It's a little joke Dad and I have between us every time we move, but this time it comes out accusing instead of funny.

"I know how you feel," he says. "Hey, I feel the same way. But this is America, Ivan. Violists are lucky to find work at all. More people like rap groups than Mozart. More people like rock music than Beethoven. More people like country music than Schoenberg."

"Hey, *I* like country music more than Schoenberg," I say through my eyedrops. Mozart and Beethoven are fine, but I like country music a lot. And as far as I'm concerned, Schoenberg is bad for the ears.

"Well, you'll hear a whole lot more country music than Schoenberg where we're going, believe me. Hey, buddy, it's people like you who put me out of work."

I half-smile through my sniffles.

"Come on. We've got to get started. You know what this means."

I nod. "Moving Mode."

Moving Mode is something you just get used to when you live with my Dad. As I say, there are not a lot of jobs in this world for people who

7

play the viola — anyway, not a lot of good ones. And Dad somehow loses the ones there are.

In Baltimore, I forget what happened. In Pittsburgh, he didn't get along with some of the other players in the chamber orchestra. In Seattle, he got along fine, but the chamber orchestra folded. And unless you're in a symphony it's hard to make enough money to live on anyway. Dad takes students, but hardly anybody really wants to learn the viola so they'll be able to not make money either, so he has to teach violin, and he doesn't really like the violin much. He calls the viola "the queen of instruments." What he calls the violin, I probably shouldn't repeat.

So I'm used to Moving Mode. Basically it involves packing all our stuff in boxes, and I am a great packer. The last two times, I packed our dishes and glassware, and not a single piece broke. Besides, it's easier as time goes on, because every time you move, there's a lot of junk you don't bother to unpack from the last time.

What doesn't get easier is the hard part of Moving Mode: saying good-bye to your friends. I kind of try to avoid all the mushy stuff — well, not mushy, exactly, but sad. It kind of takes a lot out of you when you leave your friends. I try to delay giving them the news until the very last minute.

I'm still delaying when this big manila envelope comes in the mail. It's addressed to me in half a dozen colored inks. The I's are dotted with little hearts, and around the address are palm trees and dollar signs and a very well-built woman in a bikini with a balloon over her head saying,

"Hey, Ivan!" There is also a big warning on both sides: "Do not fold, bend, or SQUASH!!!!" The return address is in Carmody, Nevada.

Inside the envelope is a videocassette — and a letter from my cousin.

> Dear Cousin,
>   I hope you're excited about your move! If you're not, you ought to be! We just can't wait to see you! You are going to love it here!
>   I thought you might want to see how great it is here, so I taped this off Channel 22! It's our Hospitality Channel, so all the tourists can see what a great place this is even when they're sitting around their hotel rooms!
>   We can't wait to see you! I'll bet you'll hardly recognize me!
>   Your *loving* cousin,
>   Gilda
>
> P.S. Be sure to check out the part about the high school!!!

Carmody is the capital of exclamation points, all right. The letter is totally dippy, but I really want to see what's on this tape. There's just one minor problem: We don't have a VCR. Dad and I talk about this a lot. He doesn't like TV. He thinks it damages your brain. He says I'm lucky we have a TV set. He says if we had a VCR, I would sit around and fry my gray matter even more than I do already.

So I decide to go across the street and try my

friend Peter Wong. He's got two VCRs and a video camera. Also a TV with the biggest screen I've seen outside of a restaurant. The first time Dad saw it, he grumbled, "Great. Brain damage for the entire family."

"Hey! Don't tell me your dad broke down and bought a VCR?" Peter says as I wave the cassette under his nose.

I scowl. "Are you kidding? *My* dad? I got a cassette, that's all."

"You planning to stare at it and wish for a VCR?"

"I'm planning," I say, "to watch it with you."

He grabs it from my hand. "No label! Hey, is it something dirty?"

"You *wish*."

"You got that right," Peter admits. It's true. Peter is the kind of guy who tapes MTV and fast-forwards to find the sexiest parts.

"This thing just came in the mail. For all I know, it could be filthy."

"Really?"

"There was a girl in a bikini on the envelope."

"All right! Maybe it *is* dirty."

"Filthy," I agree. "Look at all the dust on the outside."

Peter shoves the tape into his VCR. He grabs two remote controls — one for the TV and one for the VCR — and blasts away. The huge screen lights up with fuzz. Then the cassette kicks in and the room fills with bombastic music — the kind you hear on commercials that are trying to impress you about how great something is.

Close-up: feathers. The camera pulls back, and

10

we see more and more of a woman with a major body and nothing on it but feathers. If there are any birds left in Nevada, they have got to be endangered species.

"Freeze frame!" Peter shouts, pressing one of the buttons on the right-hand remote control. "Breast alert!"

One of the many ways I had wasted time with Peter was by single-framing through tapes of music videos, checking to see how much of women's bodies we could actually see. You'd be surprised how much you can see if you really look. Then again, maybe you wouldn't.

Anyway, this time we get to see plenty, but nothing all that special. "Come on," I say. "Fast motion again."

"Fast motion!" Peter presses the button that speeds everything up to about ten times normal. There's an aerial shot of a bunch of tall buildings with a lot of lights on them.

"Very funny."

"What is this, anyway?" Peter punches the reverse button, and everything zips by backward.

"It's the Hospitality Channel from a place called Carmody, Nevada."

The music and Ms. Feathers return in normal speed. "Who sent it to you?"

"My cousin."

Peter points to the screen. "*She's* your cousin?"

"*I* wish."

The screen cuts to the aerial shot again. This time we can hear the sound. An announcer with the kind of voice you hear in commercials is speaking in those deep tones that mean what he is saying is supposed to be REALLY, REALLY IMPORTANT.

"Ten years ago, it was only desert. Today, it's the fastest-growing destination city in the Western Hemisphere. It's Carmody, Nevada — where the lights shine bright even late, late at night. For the next half hour, we'll take you on a personal tour of our city — the miracle in the desert!"

"Give me a break." Peter hits the freeze-frame button. "No breasts here. Why are we watching this?"

"Because I'm moving there."

Peter jumps up and down on the sofa, shouting "What?"

"My Dad and I are moving to Carmody, Nevada."

"You gotta be kidding!"

I shake my head.

"Come on, Ivan! Look at this awful place!" He points to the screen. Except for the buildings and a skinny little river, it looks like desert, all right. Brown. "Why would anybody in their right mind want to go there?"

"My cousin says it's great. She says I'm gonna love it."

"Probably under the effect of locoweed. Or heatstroke. Ive, I don't believe this! Joke, right?"

"Come on. Don't you want to see the miracle in the desert?" I ask sarcastically.

Peter sighs and presses the PLAY button. The words *THE CARMODY STORY: MIRACLE IN THE DESERT* whisk to the front of the screen. An enormous pear-shaped guy with a bright red nose, a string tie, a checkered coat, and eighty-six chins fades in behind them. As it dawns on me that it's the same guy I saw on the pamphlet, the screen fills with static.

"That's it?" Peter says. "That's all she sent?"

"Fast forward it awhile," I tell him. "There's supposed to be stuff about the high school."

But there isn't. Peter remotes through the rest of the tape, but it's definitely blank.

"So here's what we can conclude," Peter says. "Carmody, Nevada, makes you so stupid you can't even make a half-hour videotape without screwing up."

"Hey, my cousin wasn't exactly a rocket scientist before she moved there."

"Locoweed. Heatstroke." Peter puts his hand on my head and turns solemn. "Farewell, future idiot. Future gerbil-brain, farewell."

And just to rub it in, he throws a surprise good-bye party for me the night before we have to leave. Everybody I know and like in the neighborhood shows up, and so do most of my friends from other parts of town. Their parents are there, too. When it's time to end the party, Peter's parents make everybody sing "Auld Lang Syne."

It's awful and beautiful at the same time. It's corny and super. It's like the end of that old movie, *It's a Wonderful Life*. It's a happy ending, but it's hard to keep from crying. I hold it in so nobody can see, or at least I think so.

Afterward, Dad and I head home for our last night in the house. Almost all our stuff is already in the van we rented, so we're using our sleeping bags. When I zip myself into mine, most of what I can see around me is the neat stuff my friends gave me for going-away presents. There are a Mariners T-shirt and sweatshirt and cap and jacket, which everybody at the party joked about being at discount, since they're out of the pennant race already. There is a major league baseball, because I am going to a minor league town. And there's a bunch of stuff for my future in the desert, like water bottles and sunglasses and a recipe for rattlesnake stew.

And me, tough, sarcastic Ivan Zellner, what do I do? I cry my eyes out, that's what.

TWO

"We're homing in," Dad says.

"We're pigeons," I grump, flapping my elbows birdwise — partly for emphasis, but mostly to dry out my armpits. We're hot and sweaty and cranky, because the air-conditioning in this rental van conked out after the first hundred miles, just in time for two solid days of hundred-degree-plus heat.

Two days ago we closed up the cargo door, put the car on the trailer hitch, swallowed the lumps in our throats, and said, "Good-bye, Seattle." We've crossed mountains and mesas and highways. We've gone through valleys and canyons and suburbs. We've seen volcanoes and arroyos and malls. We've cleaned a zooful of dead bugs and birdcrap from our windshield. Now we're in the desert. We've been there all

15

day. In case you're wondering, the desert is hot.

But at least now the sun has gone down. We can see the lights of Las Vegas blazing in the distance, but we don't even get off the freeway to investigate. Just a hundred more miles, and it's hello, Carmody, Nevada.

The lights of Las Vegas disappear behind us. The greenish twilight disappears above the mountains. As we rumble through the hot night, ours are the only lights for miles around, unless you count about a million stars overhead. Dad actually looks happy, because there's a classical music station in Vegas, and the radio is playing a Mozart quartet.

And then it starts breaking up and fading out. "Damn!" Dad shouts, "Wolfgang's gone!"

I twiddle the knob and find a country station. Hank Williams, Jr., is singing "The American Dream." He's pretty sarcastic about it, thinks it's mostly about money. From what I know, he may well be right.

"Is that the best you can do?" Dad asks.

"Classical has had it. And I like this song. You want rap? Heavy metal?"

"Silence?"

"Come on. You got your Mozart fix."

"All right. Leave it. Country. Fine."

"Speed trap," I point out. Dad grunts and slows down for a little bump-in-the-road town that's just one combination building: The Lucky Jack Casino, Coffee Shop, and Gas Station. It has an enormous Jack of Hearts on the roof.

When the speed limit gets back to normal, we

start seeing huge billboards for hotels in Car-mody. **GOLDEN SPIKE $39.95! SILVER BUL-LET $35.95 KIDS FREE! RANCHO RIO $32.95! CARMODY INN $29.95!**

"We keep going far enough," Dad says, "maybe they'll pay us to stay there."

And then we spot the turnoff and follow the arrow that says **Carmody.**

"Here we go," Dad sighs, and we head up a long, dark, winding hill that could be on another planet. All we can see are sandbanks on either side of us.

But when we crest the hill, we can see farther. Mostly what we see is an enormous American flag in lights, blazing like a beacon in the night. The radio starts playing Ricky Van Shelton's "Hole in My Pocket," which pretty much sums up our family finances.

And now we can see the rest of the sign. It's all in lights, too. Above the flag is a neon woman with bright, enormous breasts. She kicks her legs as if she's doing some sort of dance or cheer-leading routine. She does her act between an enormous pair of neon dice and a neon cham-pagne glass overflowing with bubbles. Below the flag, neon lettering says **Welcome to Carmody, Nevada — Future Entertainment Capital of the World!**

"You know, son," Dad shouts solemnly, "at moments like these, don't you truly love this country and everything it stands for?"

Phony patriotism drives him crazy. Especially when you use it to sell stuff. "We've made it,

Ivan!" he hollers, punching me in the arm. "Let's give thanks to our nation's interstate highways. God Bless America!"

Dad turns off the radio and starts in on the official lyrics to "God Bless America," singing a little too loud, a little too seriously, just to let me know this is all a big put-on. I start singing "God Bless My Underwear" instead.

We pass the sign and the road turns pitch black again. But what is that to the most patriotic singers in the U. S. of A.? Dad shifts over to my lyrics as we get to the repeat line: "God Bless My Underwear, my only pair! God bless my underwear, my . . . own . . . ly . . . pair!"

We make western-style whoops and sort of crack up. And then we see it in the distance: A town blazing with a million lights, signs that look like fireworks, and even some laser beams blasting thick rays that seem to shoot out to infinity. Carmody, Nevada.

I turn up the radio again. "You won't always win at the gaming tables," says an announcer, "but you can't lose at our dinner table. Every meal's a winner at Finger City Steak and Brew, home of the Tuesday night Double Strip — strip steak and striptease, just $4.99!"

Dad shakes his head. "Son, I do believe we have reached the Promised Land." He hands me a folded-up piece of paper. "Now all we have to do is find Penny's place."

I flip on the overhead light and unfold the page. I'm the official navigator, so it's my duty to figure out where to turn next. Unfortunately,

Penny's map looks like a diagram of a plate of spaghetti.

"More slots! More tables! More winners! More fun!" shouts the radio. "And during our Grand Re-opening, everybody wins! That's right, you get a free prize just for stopping in! The all-new Golden Spike, home of the $1.99 two-egg breakfast, served twenty-four hours a day. We're eggzackly in the middle of Entertainment Way!"

"No fair!" Dad exclaims. "They forgot to mention that I will be playing the viola at the *Girls! Girls! Girls! Revue.*"

"Damn!" I mutter, suddenly figuring out the map.

"We missed the turn?"

"Sort of. I think we're okay with the next right, though. It's just a little out of our way."

"You sure?"

"Positive. If we go straight, we're in Arizona."

Dad turns right. It's 10 o'clock on a Wednesday night, but it's bright as day on Entertainment Way. To the left there are huge hotels with enormous parking lots. To the right there's a sandhill with incredibly bright anti-theft lights and a million RVs parked under them. And straight ahead there's a traffic jam, most of it RVs and trailers and campers.

My father shakes his head. He's at least as amazed as I am. "Do you believe this?"

I'm not entirely sure I do. We're stuck at a traffic light in front of the Oasis Hotel and Casino. In front is the kind of signboard you see at movie theaters, except this one is about ten times as big as any movie sign you've ever seen. The letters are almost as tall as I am: **BEST SLOTS IN TOWN. ALL YOU CAN EAT BREAKFAST 1.49 LUNCH 2.49 DINNER 3.99. ROOMS ALWAYS AVAILABLE IF NOT WE PLACE YOU. GREAT ENTERTAINMENT IN OUR LOUNGE. RVS WELCOME.**

We crawl along past the Rancho Rio Hotel and Casino, which looks sort of Mexican, except for the colored laser beams shooting out the top. "Green, white, and red," Dad points out. "National colors of Mexico."

"Wait a minute. 'Rancho Rio' means 'River Ranch,' right?"

Dad nods.

"So how come this is the only hotel that's not on the river side of the road?"

"Probably because it wouldn't sound so great to call it 'Rancho Almost On The Rio.' "

We're still stuck at the red light. Across the road is the Cowpoke Casino and Hotel, which has a huge neon cowboy smoking a cigar. Below him, the sign says **BOUNTIFUL BREAKFAST BUFFET SERVED 24 HOURS. SENIOR SPECIALS. QUINTUPLE ODDS. SLOT SOCIETY! MORE WINNERS!**

Up ahead of the next traffic light there's a building that looks like an enormous old-fashioned railroad locomotive. It's the Golden Spike Casino and Hotel, the one we heard about on the radio, the one where Dad will be playing the viola for a bunch of birdwomen. I realize I have seen a picture of this place in one of the brochures, but you can't realize how big it is until you actually see it in person. Even from here it's huge: It looks like the world's biggest model train.

"Damnedest place I've ever seen," Dad says. "My future employer."

Eventually we get through the light. Next comes the '49er Hotel and Casino, which has old-timey beat-up mining shacks out front. Then there's the Silver Bullet Casino and Hotel, a tall round building with a sort of rocketlike nose cone on top. It's painted to look like — you guessed it.

We get stuck at another light. "I just figured it out," Dad says. "These lights are set up to stop you every time. They must figure some people will get so frustrated they'll turn into the parking lot and go gambling."

And that's when we spot the weirdest place yet. On top, the sign says **Five Stars** beneath five twinkling blue stars and **Hotel and Casino** beneath that. Right below is this enormous 3-D neon woman with five stars pasted over strategic parts of her body. Below is another enormous theater sign. It says: **FUTURE HOME OF JEE-TER P. CARMODY REGIONAL HIGH SCHOOL. 5 DAYS UNTIL THE FUTURE ARRIVES. SNEAK PREVIEW SUNDAY 9 P.M. CARMODY TIME. BE THERE OR BE SQUARE!** The buildings behind it are dark except for some worklights and flashes from welding torches.

"I don't believe this!" I really don't. "The high school is in a hotel?"

The light changes, and Dad pulls ahead. "Beats

21

me. That should be the new high school."

"In a casino? With some bimbo twirling around over it?"

Dad shakes his head. "Don't ask me. We'll get it straightened out soon enough."

Up ahead, we see the biggest sign yet. It's an enormous fat guy in a string tie. He's smiling and pointing to the hotel. Below him it says **BEST ODDS IN TOWN** and **EAT GOURMET FOR PEANUTS.** On top it says **JEETER P. CARMODY'S ORIGINAL CARMODY INN.**

"Where is the town?" Dad wonders. "All we've seen is a bunch of casinos."

"And Bimbo Regional High," I remind him.

"Let me see that map."

I hand it over as we hit another traffic light.

"Aha! All the housing is down at the south end." He points to a hill down the way, and we can see the lights of what might be houses.

We head in that direction. The lights are on houses, all right. And apartments. But it seems weird somehow. Maybe it's because there are no trees except these big old palms. Maybe it's because we haven't seen a drugstore or a super-market or even a gas station. If Carmody is in the middle of nowhere, this part of town seems like the edge of nowhere.

With the help of the map I find Corte Madre, which is the street my aunt lives on, not to mention Dad and me, after tomorrow. Half a minute later we pull up in front of number 32. The apartment complex looks sort of Mexican and doesn't have lasers coming out of the top. A sign out front says **Casa Rio**, which means River House, which is kind of optimistic, since we have got to be half a mile from the river. Apparently the river is a big deal around here.

Dad sets the brake and runs his fingers through his hair. "Well, we did it."

"We did it, all right," I say. "This just may be the worst mistake we ever made."

"We're tired, right?" Dad twists his neck around to loosen his muscles. "Let's reserve judgment till morning, okay?"

I scowl at him. "Why bother?"

"I'm not saying you're necessarily wrong. Just let's reserve judgment."

"Ha! This is one kidnapping that'll go down in history."

"Look, some people must like this place."

"Sand crabs. Desert rats."

"That reminds me. Be nice to your aunt and cousin, okay?"

I scowl and nod. As we hoist ourselves out of the cab, I hear weird animal cackles in the night. "Do tarantulas make noise?" I ask.

There's a pinch on my neck. I jump. "Only when they're biting!" Dad shrieks. We both crack up as we take our suitcases and our sleeping bags down from the cab.

Apartment number 5 is through a gate, down a walk, past a little swimming pool, and up a flight of outdoor stairs. "Pool looks okay," Dad says.

"Don't kid yourself. It's probably a mirage."

We knock on the door. It opens, and Aunt

Penny shouts, "David!" She throws her arms around my dad. The two of them jabber about how good it is to see each other.

Then she turns to me and says, "Ivan!" and it's my turn. Her hug smells like stale cigarette smoke. She says I've really grown.

I groan. "No kidding."

From inside the living room, my cousin Gilda gives me a big smile and a little wave. "Great to see you, Ivan?" She makes it sound like a question. "You are absolutely gonna love it here?"

I shrug as I step into air-conditioned comfort. I stare at her. I realize there's something different about her.

Which is weird, because I hardly remember her, except for all the makeup she wore and the time she threw up all over the kitchen table. Now she's tall and skinny and blonde, but it's pretty obvious she still spends plenty of time on her makeup. And hair. She has got a ton of it, and it sort of cascades up from her face and down her back, with a little braid on one side.

"So what do you think?" She grins at me.

Right. What's different about her is that she has a whole lot less nose. No wonder she said I wouldn't recognize her.

"Not bad," I say, staring at the middle of her face.

"Thanks." She smiles. "I'm not kidding about this town, you know? I mean, you have moved to the coolest place on earth?"

"Right. Only three hundred and eleven degrees out there."

"You know what kind of cool I'm talking about. Did you get that tape I sent you?"

"Yeah, but there was nothing on it after the beginning."

"Oh, sorry." She giggles. "I got a phone call while I was doing it? I thought I might have screwed it up." She looks at her watch. "Hey, come on. You can see it now. It's on every hour on the half hour on the tourist channel?"

She grabs my hand and drags me down the hall to her bedroom. The walls are plastered with a lot of posters of muscular guys with their shirts off.

The TV is already on, so Gilda grabs the remote and changes the channel to 22. There's a commercial with people sitting at slot machines, looking over their shoulders at the camera, and telling how much they won. The weird thing is they don't look all that happy about it. I mean, if I'd just won a thousand dollars, I'd damn sure have a smile on my face. Or even a hundred.

"It'll be on in a minute," says Gilda. "*The Carmody Story: Miracle in the Desert*. I just about have it memorized?"

"Is it going to tell me what's supposed to be so great about this place?"

"Sort of," says Gilda. "Haven't you figured it out already?"

"No," I say.

"What's so great about this place," she says, lowering her voice like a spy, "is that it's where adults come to do all the stuff they tell kids not to?"

"What's so great about that?"

"They drink? They smoke? They gamble? They stay up late? They eat till they burst? They watch people dance around naked?"

"What's so great about that?" I repeat.

"They're like not adults? They're like big kids? They're having fun? So they can't give you a load of crap about how you should behave?"

It sounds pretty horrible to me, kind of like Never-Never Land in *Peter Pan*. I mean, hey, I don't want to be a kid all my life. I want to grow up. I like adults. I like being treated with respect. I don't mind not behaving like a jerk — at least some of the time.

"Come on, cousin. Think about it. This place is really different."

"Different, yeah. Great, I'm not so sure."

Gilda flings herself on her bed, props herself on one arm, and bats her mascara at me. "Well, let me put it another way? When was the last time you were alone with a girl in her bedroom at eleven twenty-nine P.M.?"

THREE

Gilda props some pillows up against the head-board and gives me this sly smile. "Well?"

She's got me. The answer, of course, is "Never," but that seems kind of uncool, so I don't say anything.

"Well?" she repeats.

"If you want me to leave, just say so," I say. "No big deal."

Gilda laughs. "That's exactly what I'm trying to tell you. Around here, it's no big deal?" She makes a kissy face at me and points at the bed. "Now lie down? Here?"

I hesitate. "Isn't there a law about cousins?" I joke.

"What, watching TV together? Give me a break." She pats the bed impatiently.

I sit down. "Very good," Gilda says, and points

to the TV screen. I recognize the same feather-woman I saw at Peter's place, only smaller. I lean forward a little.

"Don't strain yourself," says Gilda. "You're not going to get to see anything you can't around the swimming pool."

I sort of blush. Talking about this stuff with Gilda is somehow different than talking about it with Peter. I lean back against the pillows as the aerial shot comes on and then *THE MIRACLE IN THE DESERT* stuff. The music wells up, and there's that enormous pear-shaped guy again.

"Good old Jeeter," Gilda says fondly. The bottom of the screen lights up with a line that says, *Jeeter P. Carmody*, and another line that says, *Founding Father of Carmody, Nevada*.

"There was nothing here but sand. And my dream," he explains in a southern drawl. "It was here I had my first vision. I saw a shining golden palace devoted to making plain folks happy." That was the Carmody Inn, the first hotel and casino on the banks of the Nevari River. Back then it was miles from anywhere except Finger City, and even from there people had to take Jeeter's worn-out ferryboat to get across.

"My second vision was a bridge over troubled waters," says Jeeter. Seven years ago he paid to build a bridge across the Nevari and named it after his mother. "The Winona Carmody Bridge," the announcer says, "brought new customers from Arizona and beyond. It ushered in a new era of prosperity for the Carmody Inn."

More hotels. More casinos. Now there are twelve, with two more going up. And now Carmody's got everything. There's gaming and golf and gaming and night clubs and gaming and big-name entertainment and, oh, yeah, did they mention gaming?

"In case you're wondering," Gilda says, "gaming is a classier word for gambling."

"No kidding!" I say sarcastically. "I thought it meant playing Monopoly."

Jeeter's Third Vision was the City of Carmody. When the casinos got so busy they had trouble finding workers, good old Jeeter developed what he called "The Most Beautiful City in the Entire U. S. of A."

"From what I've seen, that sounds like a wild exaggeration," I grumble.

"That's because you haven't seen anything yet, bozo," Gilda says.

This brings us to Jeeter's Fourth Vision. His Fourth Vision was what he called his American Dream. He told everybody about it at a school board meeting a couple of years ago, and now we get to see his speech on our TV screen.

"Too many of our children," he says, "finish high school without the skills they need to get ahead. For example, many of them actually graduate without ever having played a casino game or seen a first-rate magic show in person.

"And that," Jeeter explains, "is the problem. America's most important business is entertainment. It's the one export even the Japanese buy from us.

"So," Jeeter asks, "why not teach the young men and women of Carmody, Nevada, the time-honored principles of the entertainment industry? In fact, why not teach all subjects by using those principles?"

To prove how serious he was, Good Old Jeeter donated his 5 Stars Hotel to the city to become the much-needed new high school. "Now," says the announcer, "the 5 Stars Hotel has been fireproofed and is being transformed into the Jeeter P. Carmody Regional High School — a showplace like no other in the world."

"Carmody, Nevada," the announcer goes on, "is now one of America's fastest-growing cities. With the vision of great Americans like Jeeter P. Carmody, the city is on the verge of greatness. It is truly," says he as the music wells up again, "The Miracle in the Desert."

Gilda squeezes the remote control to lower the volume. She aims her new nose at me. "So what do you think?"

"I'm stunned," is all I can say.

"This high school is going to be so great! You heard: It's the only one like it in the entire world."

"Yeah. Nobody else in the world would build a high school in a hotel."

"That is what is going to be so great about it? See, the hotel was called the 5 Stars because back when it was built, Jeeter got five movie stars to put up the money, so the theme was that there were five of everything: five wings, five huge swimming pools, five theaters, five tennis areas, five gambling casinos? So the high school is divided into five separate parts?"

"I didn't see anything about that on the TV."

"The tourists don't care about the details of some high school."

"Well, I do."

"Here. Look." She reaches across me, grabs a little pamphlet from her nightstand, and drops it in my lap. The pamphlet says, *Jeeter P. Carmody Regional High School of Carmody, Nevada.* Below that it says:

The College of Performing Arts and Sciences
The College of Sporting Arts and Sciences
The College of Hospitality Arts and Sciences
The College of Gaming Arts and Sciences
The College of Comedic Arts and Sciences

"See?" she tells me helpfully. "The five parts are the five colleges. Like, I'm in Performing?"

She turns the page to show me. Performing has a picture of a guy with too much hair grease singing into a microphone and a picture of a ballerina in a dorky tutu. But that's better than Hospitality, where the pictures show two smiling women making a bed and a sleazoid guy standing under a sign that says *Registration.*

"You pick which college you get?" I ask suspiciously.

"Not exactly."

I scowl. "You mean they can say you have to learn how to make beds for a living?"

"Yeah, Hospitality does sound kind of yucko. Mom says she didn't raise me to be a waitress, which is kind of weird since that's what she is?"

I turn the page and stare at the picture under

31

Sporting. Two guys in boxing trunks are beating each other's brains out. "I'm not exactly a potential heavyweight champion."

"Don't worry. They give you a test to see where you belong. Mom got you an appointment for day after tomorrow." Gilda looks at her clock. "I mean tomorrow. It's already after midnight."

Dad sticks his head in the door. "Hey, Ive, we've got to move all our crap from the truck bright and early tomorrow. Call it bedtime?"

"Hey, Dave, this is Carmody," Gilda tells my dad. "There's no such thing as bedtime."

"Besides, it's already tomorrow, and as early as it gets," I point out.

"Perhaps we'll adapt to the local customs later on," Dad says. "Let's shower down and get some sleep."

Aunt Penny comes to the door. She is now wearing even more makeup than her daughter. "Gilda, give these guys the extra key, the one that's supposed to be in the bottom kitchen drawer? And maybe you can help them move tomorrow, so make it early, okay, like not more than two o'clock? I've got to run or I'll be late for my shift. Ivan, Dave, really great to have you here. See you later." She dashes through the front door.

Dad and I spread our sleeping bags on the living room floor. There are about a million things I want to tell him, none of them good, but I keep quiet because I don't want Gilda to overhear.

I open my suitcase and take the stuff I need into the bathroom. It's the first bathroom I've ever seen with a TV in it. The mirror is decorated with a pair of fuzzy dice on one side, a rabbit's foot on the other side, and a lucky horseshoe on top. There's a four-leaf clover on the toilet seat cover. The bath mat features the ace and jack of spades. So why is it that as I change into my bathrobe and stare at myself in the bathroom mirror, the last thing I feel is lucky?

I stare at myself. I exhale a deep breath. I make the worst face I can think of. Somehow it makes me feel better.

Then I run the tap and take a gulp of water. It tastes like rotten eggs. I mean really rotten. I spit and lean out the door. "Hey, there's something wrong with this water!"

Gilda lets out this scream that would wake the dead. She leans out her bedroom door.

"Hey, what are you screaming for?" I ask her. "*You* didn't drink it."

"You didn't drink *tap water*?" She says the words tap water the way you might say *cat vomit*.

"Yeah, I did."

"You poor boy."

"What's wrong with it?"

"You don't drink it, that's all. Ever? Didn't you see the dispenser?"

I look behind me. There's a big upside-down jug of water on a metal stand. "I thought that was for like special occasions."

"Yeah, like every time you take a sip? Our tap water's putrid? Horrible?"

"Big news."

"How much did you drink?"

"Two sips."

"Well, you *might* not get sick."

"Is it poison, or what?"

"A little minerals, a little bacteria? You may not get sick. Stick with the bottled, okay? Bottled, and down at the hotels. They've got their own filters so they won't have a lot of tourists ralphing on the slot machines?"

"Thanks," I say. "Thanks a lot."

"Don't mention it." She raises her eyebrows and stares at me. "Are you in your underwear?"

I frown and shut the door. "Thought so," Gilda hollers. "Cute."

I finish brushing my teeth. I jump in the shower. It's like showering with rotten eggs. Boy, does it stink!

"You can have the bathroom," I tell Dad when I get back to the living room. "Just don't drink from the tap."

"Why not?"

"Crazy water," I say, doing my best imitation of one of those old-time cowboy-movie sidekick geezers. "Drives you loco."

"Thanks for the warning," he says when he gets back. "You can even smell the sulfur in that stuff."

"Just one of the many wonderful features of this place," I sneer.

"You're not impressed, huh?" Dad says as he slides into his sleeping bag.

"Impressed? Ha! Hey, we're not unpacked yet. We could just get in the truck and head back home."

"Unfortunately," Dad points out, "this *is* home."

"Right. Carmody, Nevada. The Miracle in the Desert."

"That's what they call this place?"

"That's what they tell the tourists, anyway. And believe me, if I ever start liking this place, that's what it'll be, all right — a miracle."

the book. I wonder, The things I like
I could I
I haven't what day, eat for sure
I have always eat all the impact, me, and
between it. I haven't Doing the more for a
and the sure right—a sort of

FOUR

A blast of sunlight from the front window wakes
me up. Not Dad. He's still asleep on the floor,
sputtering like a chainsaw that's about to run out
of gas.

I go to the window, put my hand across my
forehead and squint out. The sun is incredibly
bright. Even the sky seems bleached out, except
for the brown part — smog. Here in the air-
conditioning, the sunlight is already hot enough
to warm me up, so it must be brutal out there
already. I wonder if Dad figured the expense of
sunscreen for this move. Of course, we won't
need much in the way of clothing.

I move back into the shadow. Down below us
is the little swimming pool, but so far nobody's
using it. A cat prowls the landing across the way.
Between buildings, I can see a couple of palm

trees and lots of sand. It's the desert, all right.

I close the curtains and get back into my sleeping bag, but there's still too much light streaming in, and I can't sleep. Besides, it's nearly eight-thirty. I decide to check out the kitchen.

There's a TV on the counter, but I leave it off because I don't want to wake Dad up. There's also a water dispenser. The refrigerator is a blizzard of coupons under magnets that look like dice and roulette wheels. I open the door. Not much in there except ketchup and eggs and milk and juice. The vegetable bins have got a couple of moldy peaches.

The action's in the freezer. It's stuffed with microwave dinners and frozen pizzas and instant waffles. I pour myself a glass of orange juice and take it out to the living room.

Dad's still sawing away. As I sit down, I sense something missing here. Then I realize what it is: There's nothing to read. Dad and I subscribe to so many magazines that sometimes we seem to be drowning in them. When we loaded up the truck, half of our cartons were books. No matter where you go into in our place, you'll find books and magazines — even in the bathroom!

But the only thing you'll find in every room here is a TV set. If there are any books or magazines around here, they're certainly well hidden. All I can find to read is the TV section of last Sunday's Las Vegas paper. That and a newspaper called *Carmody Crier*.

At least I think it's a newspaper. It looks sort of like a newspaper, but there's hardly any news in it except who's playing at the casino lounges and who won how much money at the Golden Spike and the new menu at the Rancho Rio. In fact, you can hardly tell the news from the ads, which are about how cheap the buffet is at the Silver Bullet and how big the jackpots are at the Oasis, and what hot new country act you've never heard of is at the Carmody Inn.

About the only real news I can find in the whole paper is an article headlined **Water Rationing to Continue, Says Commission,** which reports that there's a water shortage and you're not supposed to take long showers, which, considering the stench, I wasn't planning to do anyway.

There is also a picture of the ever-enormous Jeeter P. Carmody standing in front of a chain-link fence with his arm around some little bald guy. The caption says **It Won't Be Long Now.** It goes on to explain that construction work on Jeeter P. Carmody Regional High School is scheduled for completion on time, that the school will open Tuesday, that Preview Night will be Sunday, and that the little bald guy is the new principal.

Aunt Penny slips through the door, puts her finger to her lips, and disappears in the direction of the bedrooms. And for some reason, I suddenly get this awful feeling.

I am an alien here. I might as well be from outer space. I don't know beans about dice or jackpots or roulette wheels. I realize that if my cousin and my aunt weren't my cousin and my aunt, I probably wouldn't have anything to do with them.

I look back at the picture in the *Carmody Crier*. Jeeter Carmody and that little bald principal don't exactly cheer me up. It's bad enough that I hate the place I've been dragged to. What if I hate the school? What if I hate the people? What if everybody's an airhead like Gilda? The kids, the teachers, everybody?

And the manager of the apartment complex doesn't exactly make me feel welcome. Dad and I get the keys to our new place from this grizzled old guy who looks like some tough hombre out of a Western movie. His skin is the texture of an old wallet, he wears a string tie, he kind of clips off the ends of his sentences, and he's got a cigarette dangling from his lips. His office smells like it's where smoke goes to die.

We're glad to get out of there and head upstairs with our new key to our new apartment. After he gets the door open, Dad makes this grand "after you, sir" gesture, and I do the same to him. We crack up as we both step inside at once.

It is *hot* in there. Dad reaches for the air-conditioner control and cranks it up to the max. The place is your basic two-bedroom apartment, laid out like Aunt Penny's, only backwards and empty.

I check out my bedroom. It's nothing special, but it does have a view: a whole lot of desert, and off in the distance this enormous factory with huge smokestacks. But there's hardly any smoke coming out of them, which is weird, because around here I'm beginning to think smoke comes out of everything.

Including the carpets in the apartment. We

decide to deodorize them before we start moving our stuff in. And, before we can do that, we have to drive to the supermarket.

When we unhitch our car from the back of the van, Dad worries something will be wrong with the car from the long trip, but when he turns the key in the ignition, it fires right up. Man, is he glad about that! He sings the praises of Red Bunny, our ancient VW Rabbit, all the way to the supermarket tucked in a tiny shopping center a couple blocks away.

The supermarket isn't so super. It's basically an overgrown convenience store. And the prices are ridiculous. "They've got you, so they get you," Dad says, shaking his head. "Monopoly."

"You got that right," says an old guy who overhears him. "They think they can get away with it because the tourists don't know any better."

"So where else is there?" Dad inquires.

"Right across the river," says the old guy. "Finger City, Arizona. Three nice big supermarkets, take your pick. Even a mall. They've got the stores, we've got the suckers. Good luck!"

"Same to you," Dad replies. Except for the carpet stuff, a frozen pizza, a bottle of drinking water, and the most expensive six-pack of Diet Coke we have ever seen, we decide to postpone our major shopping. As we leave, the checker wishes us "Good luck."

"What's all this good luck stuff?" Dad asks.

"It's kind of a local thing?" the woman explains. "You know, 'cause you might be gambling and need it?"

"I need good luck even when I'm not gambling," Dad says. "Good luck to you, too."

Back home, the apartment has cooled down maybe a whole degree. We borrow Aunt Penny's vacuum — ours is still somewhere in the van — and get some teamwork going. Dad sprinkles the deodorizer on the carpet, and I follow behind with the machine. Since there's nothing on the floor to get in the way, it doesn't take long.

As we head down to the truck, we spot Gilda by the pool, working on her tan. Her tan isn't bad, I have to admit, but by the time she's forty, she'll probably look like that leather-skinned manager. "You busy?" Dad asks. "We could use some help."

Gilda looks as though somebody has asked her to mop latrines. "Lifting stuff?" she whines.

"We'll do the lifting," Dad says. "We need somebody to watch the truck so nobody steals anything."

Gilda gives us this big deep sigh. "You're just lucky I'm so nice." She grabs her towel, follows us out to the street, and lies down on a sunny patch of lawn across from the truck. We crack the van and begin the long move in.

As we're lugging the TV set upstairs, a guy's voice shouts from down below. "Hey, man, can I give you a hand?"

"Thanks," Dad says, half out of breath. "We're doing all right for now."

"Hey, I'll give you one anyway." The next thing we hear is some clapping from downstairs.

"Comedian," I mutter as Dad and I grunt the TV through the door.

Dad heads out for another load, but I stop to take a leak first. When I come out the front door, a tall, skinny guy is standing there. He is wearing neon pink shorts and a green T-shirt that says *Nah, I don't think so*. One of his running shoes is white, and the other one's black. But the weirdest thing about what he is wearing is a bike helmet that's surrounded by this enormous straw sombrero brim. It makes his head look sort of like a model of Saturn, except for the long, stringy hair that dangles down.

"I'm Dirk," he says, extending his hand. "Call me Greb."

I shake his hand. "Ivan Zellner."

"New around here, right?"

I nod.

"GROOVE CITY!" Greb screams. "YOU ARE GONNA LOVE THIS PLACE! THIS PLACE IS SO DREAD, MAN! WOW, IT'S BEYOND DREAD, IT'S BEYOND BAD, IT'S WARTY! NO, I MEAN, IT'S NOT EVEN JUST WARTY! IT'S PUSTULOUS. I'M TELLING YOU, MAN, IT'S RED, IT'S HOT, IT'S INFLAMED, IT'S FESTERING!"

Greb starts coughing. His gasps come in big spasms, almost like hiccups. He finally slows them down, brings them under control. " 'Scuse me," he says, touching his fingers to the brim of his sombrero-helmet as if he were tipping his hat. "Whew! Hoarse from all this YELLING!"

Dad comes up the stairs with his viola case. "Hey, what's in there, man, a machine gun?" Greb asks. "You a drug dealer?"

Dad snaps the case open. "Tune dealer."

"Hey, far out! Timbuktunian! Moonwards!"

Dad closes the case, shakes his head, and steps inside the apartment.

"Seriously, man, you really want to know about this town?" Greb asks me.

I shrug. "Sure. What's the story?"

"It sucks warm tarantulas," says Dirk Greb.

"Hey for out," Ivan murmurs. "Anyway,"

DeGusoto the care about the room, and goes inside the apartment.

"A money man, you really want to know about the town?" Gilda asks Ivan.

I direct. "Sure." "She's the man?"

"I...Ivan seems mighties," says DeGuata...

FIVE

"Hey, Greb!" Gilda shouts as she hurries up the stairs to the landing. "Cut it out!"

Greb turns his fingers into a pair of scissors.

"Don't listen to this burger, Ivan?" Gilda says. "He's got a bad attitude?"

"That's for sure," Greb agrees. "So what do you think, Ive? Want my Bad Attitude Tour?"

"No way, Dirk Greb," says Gilda. "I'm not going to let you run this place down."

"I wish somebody would," Greb says. "Like with a steamroller. Flatter than a Swedish pancake."

"That's just what I'm talking about, Dirk. You'll give Ivan the wrong idea. Just 'cause *you* don't like it."

"Me?" Greb says innocently. "Man, I *love* it here."

"Oh, right," says Gilda. "Ivan, don't hang out with this jerk? I mean, look at him?"

"Yeah, look at me, man. I'm a real slob. I'm not hip like your cousin. Insufficient mascara. Inadequate hairspray."

"Very funny," Gilda sneers.

Greb ignores her. "So you on for the grand tour, Ive? Take you around, show you the sights?"

"Sure," I say. "Why not?"

"Then I'm coming with you," Gilda declares.

Greb groans. "Give us a break! I may want to make rude remarks. I may want to do my imitation of Jeeter P. Carmody after dinner at his all-you-can-eat Pork Power buffet. I'm telling you, man, it's a gas."

I laugh. "Hey, I'd like to see that."

"See, there you go," Greb tells Gilda.

"I've seen that imitation," Gilda says, "and it stinks?"

"You do that part, too, huh?" I ask Greb.

"No, man, I'm a gentleman," he says. "I leave that part for your cousin."

"You're a laugh riot, Greb," Gilda tells him.

"I know, I know," Greb replies. "And I also know you don't want to come with us, because Mr. Laugh Riot and your cousin here are going to see the naked women down at the school."

"We are?" I say, sounding more interested than I mean to.

"Bull you are," says Gilda.

"Bull we're not," says Greb. "Naked. Women. Warty!"

"Hey, guys, I hate to interrupt anything." It's

my father, carrying a lamp up the stairs. "But could you maybe give us a little help?" He turns to Greb. "And not just that hand, friend."

"In a minute," I tell him.

Dad points to his watch. "The minute starts now." He heads through the door.

"So what about these naked women?" I ask Greb in a low voice.

"All part of the tour," Greb tells me. "All part of the tour."

"Will you give me a large personal break?" Gilda says.

"See for yourself. Come with us," Greb tells her. "You wanted to, right?"

"Forget it. If I want to see a naked woman," Gilda says, "I can look in a mirror."

Greb gives her this big smile, as if he's going to say something dirty, but he decides against it when he sees Dad come out the door. "Down by the pool when?" Greb asks me.

"Ivan, you gonna help out here?" Dad pleads.

"Yeah. Sure. How much longer you think it'll take?"

"An hour and a half, maybe? That okay with you?"

"That okay, Greb?" I ask.

"Warty!" He gives me the thumbs-up sign and heads down the stairs.

Gilda grabs my arm. "Warty is right, Ivan. You're not gonna start hanging out with that dude?"

"I'm just being friendly."

"Greb is weird? He's like a creep? He's totally antisocial?"

"No kidding?"

"Nobody can stand him?" Gilda goes on. "He's like the most unpopular person on the planet?"

I grin. "I think I'm going to like this guy."

Gilda shakes her head and puts her hand on my forehead. "Poor pitiful Ivan. You're feverish. That water must have got to you after all."

"Ivan, come on, huh?" Dad shouts. "I want to get this done. The heat's only going to get worse."

"Right!"

I hurry down the stairs with Gilda close behind. Dad's not kidding about that heat. The thermometer by the pool says 102, but it's in the shade and we aren't. I could definitely use one of those long showers we're not supposed to take, except with the water around here it probably wouldn't matter anyway.

By lunchtime the apartment looks like home — if your home has boxes of stuff all over the place and the furniture is not exactly what you'd call arranged, and none of the beds are made. Actually, Dad and I are not what you'd call great housekeepers, so in a lot of ways this really does look a lot like home, give or take all the boxes.

"I've got to take the truck in," Dad says. "You want to come with me?"

"I've got an offer for a personal tour of the town."

"With Gilda?"

"With that guy I was talking to a while back."

"No offense, but I didn't exactly like the looks of that guy. Space cadet."

"Gilda's not too fond of him, either."

"Maybe there's a reason."

"Yeah. Like she's got the brain of a gerbil."

"Just be careful, okay?"

"Hey, since when did you start worrying about the friends I pick?"

"You may find it hard to tell around here at first. I mean, *I* find it hard. People seem a little weird."

"A little!" I exclaim. "You mean like our relatives?"

"Our relatives are high on the list. No doubt about it."

"Did you know Penny plays the slot machines?"

"Ivan, everybody here plays the slot machines. They're designed to snare you in a weak moment. I'll probably be dropping quarters in them myself at the end of a long night."

"Great. My dad, a gambler. You going to start smoking, too?"

Dad grunts. "Go. Hang out. If you think he's a drug dealer or something, back off, okay?"

"Gilda hates Greb. She doesn't want me to have anything to do with him. Believe me, if he were a drug dealer, she'd've told me about it."

"What are you going to do about lunch?"

"I thought pick up a burger or something."

Dad takes out his wallet and peels off a ten. "All right, but watch it. We're on tight budget till my first paycheck, remember?"

How can I forget? We've been nickel-and-diming it all the way out here. If I see the inside of another McDonald's, I think I'll barf Egg McMuffins.

I go down to the pool. Nobody is there but

Greb, and when I look at the thermometer it's pretty clear why. It's still in the shade, but it now reads 106.

Greb is in the shade himself. He's reading a book about global pollution. He's abandoned his Saturn helmet for an enormous regular sombrero. "Zellner! You got a car?"

I shake my head. "I don't even know how to drive."

"Suppurating! What, are you some kind of ten-year-old? Big for your age?"

"Fifteen-and-a-half," I answer. "So where's your great car?"

"Down at the dealer's," he says. "Until I turn sixteen and buy it. Great, man. Two wheelless wusses. Great."

"What does suppurating mean, anyhow?"

"Like oozing pus?"

"Pustulous? Same thing?"

"Close. Full of festering pimples."

"Quite a vocabulary."

"What can I tell you? My dad's a doctor."

"What kind?"

"The kind that wouldn't set foot in this town if you paid him. Surgeon. Brain. Lives in Maine."

"So you live with your mom?"

"Hey, wait a minute," Greb says. "I'm asking the questions here."

"So-o-o-o sorry."

"Pretty good Willsman imitation. You like the guy?"

"Is there anybody who doesn't?"

"Me."

"I should've guessed."

"Too many cheap laughs with that green face. Too easy."

"Funny, though."

Greb sighs. "You and a hundred million other morons think so. Where you from, anyhow?"

"Seattle. And a whole bunch of places before that."

"Where's your mom?"

"My Dad and I wouldn't mind knowing that. Hey, are we going to tour this town or do I have to go talk to Gilda?"

"Hey, man, chill a little, okay? You move too fast in this heat, you wind up fried."

I push a lounge chair from the sun into the shade. I sit down. I jump up again. That chair is *hot!*

"So what about your mom?" Greb presses.

"She cut out with some guy about six years ago. We get a Christmas card from her every year. It's always from somewhere different."

"I see a fixup in the making, man."

"What, your mom and my dad?"

He jumps at me and gives me a bearhug. "Brother!"

I give him this look. Maybe Gilda is right. Maybe this guy is out of his gourd.

He steps back and laughs. "Kidding, man. Just kidding."

"What does your mom do?"

Greb grins. "Dances." He grins wider. "Naked."

"She must have a . . ." I suddenly blush.

"Yeah, great body. Great." He can see the look on my face. "Well, she doesn't dance *totally* naked.

There's a law against total nudity in this town."
He raises his voice. "Except where we're going,
man! I told you we are going to see naked women,
and that's what we're going to see!"

"You sure about this?"

"Hey, why shouldn't I be? This is cold, man.
This is ice. This is absolute Antarctic zero! Naked!
Totally!"

"Where are we going to see these women?"

"Where you think, dude? At the site of our
future educational conquests."

"What, the high school?"

"Jeeter P. You-Know-Who Regional You-
Know-What. Rah. Rah. Blah. Blah," he chants
like some cheerleader with a bad case of sleeping
sickness. "Carmody! Carmody! Carmody High!"
he shouts, sarcastically pronouncing it Car-MOE-
dee. Then he corrects himself, almost: "Excuse
me: Comedy High!"

"Is that what everybody calls it?" I ask.

"Everybody who's hip. Go Volcanoes," he says
wearily.

"Volcanoes?"

"Team nickname."

"What? There aren't any volcanoes anywhere
near here."

"Another mystery to be revealed on our tour,
my son."

I scowl. "Naked women, huh? All over the
place? At the high school?"

"Man, are you a nuke, or what?"

"Nuke?" Greb's slang is beginning to get ir-
ritating.

"Nuke. Newcomer. We get 'em all the time.

Hey, it's okay. I mean, if you're from a normal part of this planet, which you are, sort of, you would say to yourself, 'How in the world could naked women be all over the place at a public high school?' I understand, man. I do. But, hey, naked women are a part of the history of the Jeeter P. High. So are drinking, gambling, drugs, destruction, and death. I mean, our high school symbol could well be, hey, I don't know, a skull and crossbones with a naked woman dancing on top of it and pulling the handle of a slot machine while the flames of hell lick up at her."

I just stand there, more or less stupefied. At most I have half an idea of what Greb is talking about.

He looks at his watch and takes a deep bow. "After you, oh confused one. Our chariot awaits."

SIX

A wait is right. Greb and I stand around for about twenty minutes broiling beneath the little sign that says "Carmody Car Stop." Shade? Forget it. Number 25 sunscreen and my Seattle Mariners cap are the only things between me and terminal redness.

And some chariot! What finally pulls up is this little beat-up minibus that's decorated to look like an old-fashioned trolley. At least the air-conditioning works. The cold hits us with its mercy the second the door opens.

"You got two bucks?" Greb asks as we get on. I dig into my pocket and come up with two singles. Greb grabs them from me and sticks them in the box.

"Another fine feature of Carmody, Nevada," he says as we sit down. "These things are free as long as you're just going between the casinos. To or from town, it's a buck each way."

"In other words, tourists are more important than people who live here."

"Please!" Greb says indignantly. "Don't call them tourists. How undignified."

"What am I supposed to call them?"

"Suckers. Call them suckers."

I frown.

"Well, not to their faces. But hey, man, suckers are more important than anything. Suckers stop coming, this place is dead meat. History. A ghost town. Toast. We love suckers. We worship suckers. We idolize suckers. Yes sir, Mr. Sucker — I mean Mr. Tourist, sir, anything you want, your highness, sir. Yes, sir, good luck, sir, you BIG DUMB *SUCKER!*"

I point out the window as I crack up. "What's that?"

"What's what?"

"That building with all the smokestacks." It's the one I can see from my bedroom window.

Greb doesn't even turn to look. "That, my friend, is the Nevazona Generating Station. It is the world's fifteenth-largest coal-fired electrical power plant. It is the law of our fair city that whenever you pass it, you as an official resident and non-sucker must say 'That's Carmody, all right: fifteenth-rate all the way.' "

"That's Carmody. Fifteenth-rate all the way," I repeat, taking another look. "Doesn't that thing give off a lot of pollution?"

"Pollution? Not a bit, my boy. Jeeter P. Carmody says so himself. You see anything coming out of those stacks?"

"No."

"That's why." He points to a huge dump truck up ahead.

"I don't get it."

"That's an ash truck. They collect the crap the plant's stack scrubbers take out of the air. The official joke for this part of the ride is, 'Better get *your* ashes hauled.' "

"I don't get that either."

Greb throws up his hands. "Hey, man, where you been?"

"Elsewhere?"

"You never heard about getting your ashes hauled back there in Seattle?"

"No," I admit.

Greb makes a face. "It's black slang. It means, you know — *doing it.*"

"Doing what?"

Greb doesn't say anything. He just stares at me.

I suddenly get it. Man, can I be thick sometimes! "Did you make this up?"

"No need, man. I read."

"Where'd you read that?"

"*Dictionary of American Slang.* Wentworth and Flexner. I'll show it to you sometime."

"Sounds okay."

"Better than okay. It's warty! Cold! Frigorific! Hey! Wait! Whoa! GETTING OFF!" he shouts, banging on the call button as he stands up. "And now we descend to Entertainment Way, home of the casinos. Not to mention our beloved future high school."

We step out of the bus into the inferno. "Man! Be lucky if my shoes don't melt!"

"Been known to happen," says Greb. "Let's get us some A.C."

"What's that smell?" I ask.

"Smell? What smell?"

"Kind of like rotten eggs."

Greb grins and holds his nose. "Wedcome to Edertainment Way."

"Whew! It stinks! What is it?"

Greb lets his nose go. "Nevazona. High-sulfur coal. The scrubbers get the ash out, but they don't get all the sulfur."

"God! Is it like this all the time?"

Greb smiles. "Only when the wind's blowing this way."

"Man, I'm glad of that!"

"False," Greb says. "When the wind blows the other way, we get the stench down where we live." Greb sees the disgusted look on my face. "What did I tell you, man? Warm tarantulas. *Stinky* warm tarantulas."

We have crossed an enormous outdoor parking lot and made it to the shade of a huge parking garage. We are heading for the front of the Silver Bullet Hotel by the only halfway cool route.

"I thought we were going to see naked women," I protest.

"In time, man, in time," says Greb. "You ever been in a casino?"

"I thought you had to be twenty-one."

"Well, you do, sort of. And you don't. Come on."

Greb leads the way. As we near the front door, he points toward the parking lot. "Check out the handicapped spaces."

There's nothing special about them, but I see what he means. There have to be two dozen of them, more than I've ever seen in one place. And there are cars in most of them.

One old man is helping his wife get out of their car. They each have one of those metal walkers.

"Is there a special deal for the handicapped?" I ask Greb.

"Nothing special about it. Just prunies."

"Prunies?"

"Wrinklies. Ancients. Senior Citizens. Golden Agers." Greb sucks in his cheeks. "Watch. That's what you'll see here more than anybody else. Old people. You'd think there was a miracle cure here or something. The Fountain of Festering Pustulous Youth."

"Ponce de Leon." I say. "The Fountain of Youth was supposed to be in Florida."

"Well it sure as shoot isn't here, 'cause I don't see any of 'em leaving any faster than they came in." He points to an elderly couple hobbling out with their canes. "But, man, that doesn't stop 'em! They come in their cars. They come in their RVs. They come pulling trailers. They come on buses. They come on the ferryboats. They jam up traffic on Entertainment Drive and bend fenders in the parking lots. After you, *mon ami*."

Greb holds the front door open for me. A sign just inside says you have to be twenty-one to enter the casino and all minors will be prosecuted to the fullest extent of the law. "What about that?" I ask.

"No problem. Don't worry about it. We're not actually going into the casino. Trust me." Suddenly he stops short and waves his arm grandly in front of us. "Look."

"Holy . . . I don't know what." It's the damnedest thing I have ever seen. It's this enormous room with slot machines stretching as far as you can see. There are tinselly lights everywhere. Lighted signs flash words like **JACKPOT!** and **CASH!** and **WIN!** and various gimmicky amounts of money, like **$3456.78!** and **$7777.77!**

And the noise! The machines whir and sirens whine and people holler and coins tinkle and crash. Every couple of seconds a new sound erupts. No matter where you look, something big seems to be happening all the time. I guess that's the idea, to make you think so.

Ten feet in front of me, there's a grandmotherly little woman with a baseball cap that says "Old Fart." She is sitting at a slot machine, grabbing handfuls of quarters that are bouncing into the payoff bin, stuffing them into big plastic cups. But she doesn't look happy about it. It's as though it's almost a chore. She finishes filling the cup and takes a drag on her cigarette.

"They're all here just to gamble? Just to win money?" I ask.

"Win money, pass the time. Keeps them off the streets."

"Amazing," I say.

Greb shakes his head. "Church," he says. "It's church. First Tabernacle of the Almighty Dollar. They come in and go straight to the change window for huge cups full of quarters. They feed the machines and pull the handles all day long. They smoke, they drink and, when their arms get tired from pulling the handles, they take a break for a gut-buster at one of the all-you-can-eat buffets. I guess it's Prunie Paradise. Here we go."

He grabs my arm and yanks me off to the right. We go up a flight of stairs to a balcony that looks out over the entire first floor. Down below us, people are shooting dice — craps, Greb informs me. Further away, people are playing blackjack and poker. They're betting on a big wheel of fortune and roulette wheels like the ones I've seen in spy movies. And of course, they're pulling the handles on about half a million slot machines.

"You sure it's okay to be here?" I ask Greb.

"Positoonly."

"What about that sign?"

"It's like it always is for kids. You're allowed to look. You're allowed to watch. You're allowed to get a taste for it. You're just not allowed to do it till you're twenty-one. See that carpet down there — where it changes from gold to red, where the slot machines start?"

"Right."

Greb points. "See that big guy with the gun?"

"Yeah."

"Okay. As long as we stay on the red carpet,

everything's fine. We step on the gold, the big guy with the gun comes over and has a little chat with us."

I look at my feet. The carpet under them is red, so I guess we're okay, but that gun makes me a little nervous.

"You know how this works, right?" Greb asks.

"Sort of." Dad has explained casinos to me, but I'm willing to listen to Greb's version.

"Basically, the deal is that the casinos know the odds," Greb explains. "Like if you throw a coin, it'll come up heads half the time."

"Right."

"Wait a minute. Check this out." Greb points to a woman with carrot-colored hair straight from a bottle. She's standing in front of a slot machine and screaming, "I won! I won!" at the top of her lungs. A siren is going off, and the lights flashing on her machine make it look like the top of a cop car chasing somebody.

"Well, at least somebody's excited about winning," I say.

"Yeah! Warty!" Greb agrees. "Where was I? Oh, yeah. If you bet a dollar it'll come up heads, but if it comes up tails, you lose and you pay the dollar, right?"

"Right."

"So what's fair would be the same for the house, the casino, who you're betting against. If it does come up heads, they lose, they pay you a dollar. Still there?"

I'm not paying absolutely strict attention. Some guy down below us at the craps table has just tossed ten hundred-dollar bills out on the green felt. A guy in a string tie — a dealer, Greb says — changes them into ten red plastic chips. I suddenly realize there are a whole lot of those red chips out on the table — thousands of dollars being gambled at once. I wonder what you have to do to be able to do that.

"Okay," Greb goes on. "You pay a dollar if you lose, right? We've established that. Well, instead of paying you a dollar if you win, the casino only pays you like ninety cents. Maybe ninety-five. That's how they make their money. They take what's coming to them when you lose, but they hold a little bit back when you win."

I shake my head. "Who'd take a bet like that?"

Greb sweeps his hand across the room below us. "Everybody down there."

"Wow," I say. "Who said getting older made you wiser?"

"Parents, man. Had to be. Hey. Whoa. Check." He points straight down.

I look. Directly below us is this blonde with a tray of drinks. She's serving them to the guys at the craps table. Her dress is cut so low on top you can see just about everything. It's not the kind of dress you see schoolteachers wearing every day.

"Nice view, huh?" Greb says. "Look out there. There are probably two dozen women wearing those dance-hall hostess outfits. They're almost as skimpy on the bottom. Not bad. Unless you're the one who has to wear the outfit to make a living."

I look. Greb is right. "So are these the naked women you promised?" I feel slightly cheated, but only slightly.

Before Greb has a chance to answer, a female voice behind us says, "Caught you!" I turn around. It's a girl about our age, a girl in a short-skirted cowgirl outfit that isn't low-cut but manages to emphasize her breasts, which are on the large size. Somehow, though, you don't think of cowgirls as wearing glasses. Or being black. "What are you doing, Greb?" she asks.

Greb actually blushes a little. "I'm showing off the sights of our fair city. A nuke." He points to me.

"Does this nuke have a name?" asks Annie Oakley. I notice her Silver Bullet badge says *Cait* and *Baltimore*.

"Ivan Zellner," Greb says, pointing. "Caitlin McKibbin."

"Why, Mr. Zellner, welcome to the Silver Bullet. I hope I can be of assistance," she says with a sugary phony cowgirl accent. She makes this very overdone curtsy and extends her hand to me, kind of dangles it in front of my nose.

Greb grunts. "What, is he supposed to kiss it or something?"

Apparently. Caitlin sighs and withdraws her hand. "Where you from, Ivan?"

"He's from the Great Northwest," Greb puts in before I can open my mouth. "Mountain man. Logger. Paul Bunyan. Just moved in today."

"Greb, does he have a voice, or do you do all his talking for him?"

"Hey, I can talk," I say. "He's right. I'm new around here."

"What grade?"

"Same as us," Greb says.

Caitlin cocks a finger-gun in Greb's direction. "Greb, would you please butt out a minute?"

"Wart," Greb croaks, and turns back toward the casino floor.

"Are you from Baltimore?" I ask Caitlin. "I used to live there."

"Me, too," she says.

"You remember the Inner Harbor?"

"You kidding? We moved to Vegas when I was two."

I point to the badge. "False advertising?"

Caitlin shrugs. "Nobody's allowed to be from around here. It's supposed to impress the suckers."

"The outfit, too, right?"

"Corny, but what can you do? All part of the authentic Western atmosphere. It's the uniform for Western Wonders."

"Western Wonders?"

"Just a dumb gift shop." She twirls around. "Yahoo," she says sarcastically. "Yippee. The suckers are supposed to love it."

"Do they?"

She shrugs. "You'd be *amazed* at all the crap we sell. Authentic western jewelry made in Taiwan. Authentic western beer mugs made in Malaysia. Authentic western baseball caps made in Singapore." She makes a face. "What do you think about the high school?"

I shrug. "All I know so far is what I saw on the tourist channel."

Greb starts humming the theme from *Jaws*.

"Yeah, it's going to be weird. Double weird. Maybe triple weird," she says. "Hey, you looking for a job?"

"Forget it," Greb mutters to me. "You don't have the legs for a cowgirl."

"Very funny," Caitlin tells him. "You'll have to do better than that if you expect to pass comedy."

"Comedy?" I say.

"Five divisions in the high school?" Caitlin reminds me. "Comedy's one?"

"Oh, yeah," I say.

"Colleges," Greb corrects her. "They're called colleges."

"Well so-o-o-o sorry," Caitlin says.

"Hey, a Willsman fan!" I exclaim.

"You bet." Caitlin smiles. "Anyhow, Greb got assigned to the College of Comedy. That's where they put all the bozos."

"So where are you?" Greb sneers. "Sports! What are you going to learn, how to dribble?"

"We'll see who learns what, Mr. Chuckles," Caitlin says. "Anyway, Ivan, what about that job? No comments from Comedy College."

"What kind of job?" I ask.

"Any job in the hotel, almost," Caitlin says. "You can't work in the casino till you're twenty-one. You could work in the gift shops, the restaurants, the video center. We're always hiring."

"Because they don't pay diddly," Greb says.

"Nobody pays diddly in Carmody," Caitlin answers. "At least here you get meals. I guess you're getting rich moving boxes around at the market."

"On my way to my first billion," Greb says over his shoulder.

"Look, Ivan," Caitlin says, "if you do decide you want a job down here, give them my name and then let me know, okay? I get a bonus for every person I bring in. It's called the Bounty Hunt?"

"Nice to know you care," Greb mutters.

"Listen, I've got to get back from break," Caitlin says. "Great to meet you, Ivan. Think about that job. And don't hang around with this weasel too much. He'll warp your mind!" She takes off down a hallway behind us.

"In case you didn't figure it out, that was Caitlin," Greb explains.

"She seems okay."

"Her chest definitely is. Maybe someday she'll wear something like that." He points down below. We can see down the top of another one of those dance-hall hostess costumes. The hard-faced woman looks up and gives us a dirty look. One of the dealers does the same thing.

"Whoops. Time to retreat. May as well see the rest of this palace."

We head down the hallway that's right behind us. It's easy to tell the employees from the suckers, because the employees have badges and wear some form of western outfit. We pass a bunch of restaurants — everything from an ice cream stand to all-you-can-eat buffets to expensive fancy steakhouses. Every one has some kind of dumb western theme.

We grab burgers at Steer Country. It's your basic fast-food joint, except the people behind the counter wear cow suits, and when your burger comes out they whomp it with a little Circle SC branding iron. Cute.

After lunch, we head out past a bunch of little shops that sell stuff like horrible paintings of cowboys. When we pass Western Wonders, Caitlin is standing with a little old lady who's buying three ten-gallon hats. Cait waves at us. I wave back. Greb puts his hands in his ears and wiggles them at her. Cait holds her nose.

Greb and I go back downstairs and head outside. The heat slams into us like a brick wall. A hot brick wall.

And then I hold my nose. "Does it stink worse out here," I ask, "or is it me?"

"If it is you, you must have cut the worst one of all time. Pus-tu-lous! Whew!"

SEVEN

"Is there *anything* good about this place?" I ask.

"Yeah, if you're a cactus," Greb says.

"The high school?" It's just across the street, but Greb is leading me in the opposite direction. "Those naked women?"

"Patience, lad. Patience."

I need it. As we head across the Silver Bullet parking lot, heat waves rise from the concrete and nail me in the gut. I feel like a prunie myself; the heat is drying me out and shriveling me up.

But Greb insists on showing me every last casino on Entertainment Way. That would be okay except for getting from one to the next. It's a tough choice: Wait for the Carmody Car and broil, or walk across the parking lot and roast. It is *hot* out here. And smelly. At least it's air-conditioned when you finally get inside a building.

Every one of the casinos has a theme. Western is the most popular. The Silver Bullet and the Cowpoke go in for cowboy outfits. At the '49er, the guys wear these miner outfits, right down to lights on their caps. The Golden Spike is big on railroad stuff from the old days. Everybody there wears engineer's caps.

The Rancho Rio is fake Mexican. When you ask somebody a question, you always get the answer, "*Si, señor.*" Greb's sombrero fits right in. In fact, that's where it comes from, a souvenir of some contest.

At the Oasis, the theme is the desert. The dealers wear Arab headdresses, and the cocktail waitresses have belly-dancer costumes, right down to fake jewels in their bellybuttons.

Then there's Jeeter P. Carmody's Original Carmody Inn, where the theme is "tackiness." The place is beat-up, falling apart. The handle is loose on the door. Stuffing pops out of the seats at the slot machines. The employees wear uniforms with stains on them. The casino is so dark you couldn't see the decorations if there were any, which there aren't. And it's so smoky in there, you can't even see the blue haze, because the second you come through the door, you're in it. "What a dump!" I say.

Greb smiles. "Yeah. But this is the busiest dump of them all."

I glance around the casino. He has a point. In the other places, there are empty seats at the slot machines. Here, every machine has a tourist in front of it. "Why would they come here when they could go to the other places?"

"Cheapest rooms in town," Greb says. "Cheapest food. And once you're here, why go out in the heat? At least this place is real."

"It's real, all right. Real sleazy."

"Hey, haven't you figured it out yet?"

"Figured what out?"

"It's the whole point of my tour."

"What is?"

"Listen up, your pustulousness! A slot machine is a slot machine. A casino is a casino. They're *all* sleazy. The rest of them just try to pretend they're not. That's what this town is all about, man: pretending it's something it's not."

He's right. The themes and the decorations kind of hide it, but even though all the casinos seem different, they're more or less the same. The only real differences are the themes — and maybe how low they cut the cocktail waitresses' blouses and how high they cut their skirts.

"There is one thing to understand about this town," says Greb. "They can call it a miracle, but that's not what it is. It's a mirage, is what it is. And now we're going to see the biggest mirage of all."

"The naked women."

"No man, they're for real. I'm talking about that phantom place of education, that imaginary molder of our future, the Jeeter P. C. R. H. S."

As we step outside, a Carmody Car pulls up, so we grab it and ride exactly one block. Hey, it's free as long as we don't go home.

"LEARNING CITY, MAN!" Greb shouts as

69

we step out. "DREAD! INFLAMED! SUPPU-RATING! (Can I skip the rest, Ivan? I'm getting hoarse again.)"

We are standing in front of the chain-link fence under the sign that says **Jeeter P. Carmody Regional High School.** It's the same sign I saw last night, except now the huge letters say **4 MORE DAYS TILL THE FUTURE BEGINS.**

"Will you please explain something?" I ask Greb.

"What am I here for?"

"Okay. This is not a hotel any more, right? The whole place is gonna be the high school, right?"

"Right with stars on."

"So how come they kept the top of the sign? You know, the part that says **5 Stars Hotel and Casino?** And the, uh . . ."

"Bimbo with the star outfit?"

"Yeah."

"Man, that's The 5 Stars Gal. She's a hysterical landmark."

"What?"

"There's supposed to be a plaque here to prove it. See, there was a big deal about her. At the council meetings, some people said the sign was, like, inappropriate and sexist. A *lot* of people said that, actually. But then Jeeter P. Carmody got up there with a tear in his eye, and he said that this town may not have a lot of history, but The 5 Stars Gal was the first really big neon sign in town, and she's been a landmark for over nine years, and you shouldn't tear down your heritage and sacred trust, and before you could say 'Jeeter

P. Carmody,' the council passed a law declaring the sign a historical landmark."

"Why?"

"Hey, like three-quarters of the people on the council work for Carmody Classic Enterprises. You think they're going to vote against their boss? Besides, you gotta understand, this place really is historical. The 5 Stars was the second hotel in Carmody. It was named after five famous movie stars you've never heard of. And about a year after it went up, the 5 Stars had a famous fire where thirty-two not-so-famous-people met famous deaths, and, surprise, no one wanted to stay there anymore. They changed the name of the hotel a couple of times, but that didn't really fool anybody. Hey, the whole reason Jeeter gave this joint to the city in the first place was because it went broke and just sat here."

"So you're telling me we're going to school in a firetrap?"

"Former firetrap. They haven't had a fire in here in like six years, if you don't count some of the fire-eating magicians."

"Great."

"And they fireproofed it, man. At least that's what the school board said when everybody protested about sending their kids here."

"Great," I say. "I'm going to a high school that features Hospitality and Comedy and may burn down any second."

"Be an optimist. Maybe it'll burn down right before that big test you forgot to study for."

"Sure. About as likely as seeing these naked women you promised."

Greb looks puzzled. "Hey, you're right. This is weird. They were right out here yesterday. Other side of the fence."

The heat is making me kind of irritable. "Hey, man, it's hot out here. Don't pimp me."

"Truth," he says, holding up his left hand. "Honest. Maybe they're down this way now."

We walk down the road toward the river. We dodge a couple of big trucks hauling construction equipment and debris. Then I notice something weird through the fence.

"What's that thing?" I ask.

"What thing?"

"That enormous bulgy thing. Under that tarp?"

"You remember you were wondering why the school's team nickname is the Volcanoes?"

"Yeah."

"Well, you're staring at it."

"What?"

"Under that tarp, pal. The world's third largest man-made volcano."

"You're kidding."

"It's been out of commission since the hotel went broke."

I can't quite believe this. "It erupts?"

"No, man," Greb says sarcastically. "It just sits there."

"No kidding. It erupts, huh? You ever see it?"

"Sure. Plenty of times."

"And?"

"Hey, it's not all that different from other man-made volcanoes."

"Like you've seen others!" I snort.

"Hey, dude, there's one in Vegas. Goes off every fifteen minutes. It's like an enormous fountain with big sprays of water, and then these huge flames shoot up from the middle. Stops traffic for blocks. Proves Americans can waste precious natural resources for silly reasons. I mean, there was a whole big deal about whether they should put this one back in working order."

"Don't tell me," I say. "Historical landmark."

In the middle of giving me a "you got that right" look, Greb suddenly lets out a war whoop. "Fast!" he shouts. "Check it out! Here they come! Last chance!"

"What?"

"NA-KED WO-MEN!!!!!"

Greb spins me around toward a truck coming at us. As it approaches, I can see what he's talking about — on the loadbed in back are the forms of a bunch of naked women. Except they're really big, dusty naked women. "*Statues* of naked women?" I shout. "Greb!"

"Hey, how often do you see breasts this big?" Greb hollers as the truck roars past us.

"Or women?" I shout as it turns on Entertainment Way.

Greb stares longingly at the concrete bodies as the truck disappears. "Pretty amazing, huh?"

"Not exactly what I was expecting," I tell him.

"Come on. You didn't exactly expect live human beings with their clothes off, did you?"

"Well, I was kind of hoping," I admit.

"Son, it's that kind of attitude that keeps my mom in business. Hey, think about it. Those statues used to be all around the casino. The

73

pools, too. Would've made for an interesting swim class, huh?"

"Maybe they should've made the statues historical monuments," I suggest.

"Damn!" Greb slaps his forehead. "Why didn't I think of that?"

EIGHT

There are no naked women back home at our pool, but a couple of their outfits come pretty close. Now that the pool's in the shade, people are actually hanging out there. Little kids are wading with their parents at the shallow end. Older kids are horsing around in the middle. A couple of prunies are snoozing in the sun on the patio. And down at the far end, a couple of girls are doing their fingernails and giggling. I just know my cousin Gilda has to be one of them.

"Hey, Ivan!" she calls as Greb and I start up the stairs. "Ivan! Over here!"

We go over. She doesn't look too terrible in her bathing suit, though you can tell she isn't about to go into the water and mess up fifty dollars worth of makeup. "You may go now," Greb," she says. "I didn't call you."

Greb grins. "That's why I'm here."

She points one wet fingernail toward the next lounge chair over. "Ivan, that's Wendy."

Except for her dark hair, Wendy could be Gilda's clone, right down to the cute little nose. "Hi," I say, wondering if they share the same plastic surgeon.

Wendy is waving her fingernails in the air to dry them, but she stops long enough to shade her eyes from the sun to see if I look okay. She smiles back at me and says hi. Then she makes a face as though she's seen a tarantula. "Oh. Greb."

"How was the tour?" Gilda asks me with a snotty tone and a flurry of fingernail waving.

"I survived," I say.

"Did you see the high school?" Gilda asks.

Greb nods. "Naked women."

"Isn't the school going to be awesome?" Wendy squeals.

"The volcano will, at least," I say.

"Come on, Ivan. Don't you think it's going to be totally great?" Gilda pushes.

"Excuse me while I puke," Greb says before I get a chance to answer. He sticks out his tongue, puts his finger on it, and makes this barfing sound: "*Bleaaaaah!*"

"Dirk, will you give us a large personal break?" Gilda complains.

"Hey, give *me* one. When anybody tells me something is going to be great, I know I'm being hustled. Advertising tells me stuff is going to be great. Television tells me stuff is going to be great. You know what I'm talking about, Ive?"

"Sort of." Following Greb's thought processes is not always the easiest thing in the world.

"Yes, you do. I mean, how many movies have you seen that were supposed to be great, but stank? How many TV shows have been hyped to the skies and then turned out to be totally lame? Excuse me, but when somebody tells me something is going to be great, my personal built-in automatic crap detector kicks in."

Gilda ignores him. "Did you see this, Ivan?" She points to a neon-pink pamphlet on the table beside her. "Go ahead. Pick it up. I don't want it to stick to my nails."

I pick it up. *BE THERE OR BE SQUARE!** scream the words on the front. Down below, in tiny print, it says, *or in deep, deep doo-doo.*

"Hot, huh?" Wendy says.

"Whoop! Whoop! Whoop!" Greb screams like a car alarm that's gone berserk. "Crap detected! Form: 'Hot!' An even bigger hustle than 'Great!' "

Gilda gives him a dirty look. "Dirk, could you like shut up for like fifteen seconds?"

"Hey, better than that. Got stuff to do. Poof! I'm gone. See you, dude." Greb pats me on the back and takes off up the stairs.

Gilda gives him a sarcastic little good-bye wave. "What a lame," she mutters. Wendy rolls over on her front.

"Will you just take a look at this, Ivan?" say Gilda's lips as she coats them in purple. "Please?"

I look again. "What is this?"

"Orientation material. From high school."

"Come on. No high school sends out letters that say 'Be there or you're gonna be in deep you-know-what.' "

"That's what I'm telling you? That's why I think it's got a chance to be totally ex?"

"Ex?" I say with a sarcastic tone. *Ex* is one of those slang words that you only see in girls' magazines. It's short for excellent. "High school is going to be totally *ex*?"

"Totally."

"More like partially ex. Sort of ex. More not-ex than ex," I say.

Gilda is getting exasperated. "Will you please read this? Like from the front?" She grabs the pamphlet, flips it over, and stuffs it into my hands again.

Jeeter P. Jive is what it says at the top of the page. *Official Orientation News from JPCRHS*. Below that, there's a picture of fifty people standing underneath The 5 Stars Gal. They are all making the thumbs-up sign, but that isn't what's weird about the picture. Every one of the thumbs-up people is wearing some kind of costume or uniform, everything from a magician's cape to football gear, but that's not what's weird about the picture. What's weird about the picture is that every single person in it is wearing nose glasses — you know, those huge false noses with big glasses and floppy moustaches. Below the picture is a caption that says "The faculty knows. The staff knows."

It's so ridiculous that I actually grin a little. Gilda picks up on it. "Yeah, right. Not bad, huh?"

I want to say something about Gilda's nose,

but I decide to restrain myself, so I don't say anything.

The rest of the page just says *WE'RE READY! You can be, too: Check out the numbers inside!*

I turn the page and see *THE OFFICIAL DRESS CODE OF JEETER P. CARMODY REGIONAL HIGH SCHOOL.*

"Yeah, right." I scowl at Gilda. "A dress code. Totally ex."

Gilda rolls her eyes. "Will you just read it?"

I look at the page. The word *TOPLESS* is in the middle of a big red circle with a slash through it. The word *BOTTOMLESS* is in the middle of a big red circle with a slash through it. Then there's a circle with no slash through it. Inside that one are the words *You're on your own, dude.**

That seems to be the entire dress code, except for what it says down at the bottom in tiny letters: **The athletic staff politely requests gentlemen and ladies to bring appropriate support garments. But, hey, it's not our personal equipment at risk. Just don't say we didn't warn you.*

I smile and shake my head. Maybe Gilda is on to something. Or maybe not: The next page says *ITEMS BANNED FROM THE JPCRHS PREMISES.* There's a list below it:

GUNS other than squirt.

KNIVES that can cut through cafeteria spaghetti in less than five tries.

OTHER WEAPONS not including pens, which have been known to be rather powerful. Please save fists for boxing class.

DRUGS stronger than coffee or cola (except with doctor's prescription); love, however, is exempt.

CIGARETTES, CIGARS, PIPES, SNUFF, CHAW and other tobacco paraphernalia (even with undertaker's prescription).

INTOLERANCE except for intolerance.

PREJUDICE except against prejudice.

PRECONCEPTIONS Hey, this school is new! We're not starting with outmoded rules.

"See?" says Gilda. "You ever hear of a high school that ever did anything like this?"

"*Aiieee!*" That loud scream keeps me from answering. Next thing I know, I'm yanked straight up off the ground. Some guy has me in a half nelson. Or maybe it's a full nelson. I mean, I'm not exactly an expert when it comes to the Nelson family. The only ones I'm sure of are Ozzie and Harriet.

"Hey!" I shout. "Let go!" I try to break free, but whoever's behind me is obviously an expert at body holds.

"He does this to everybody?" Gilda tells me. "It's his way of saying hello?"

"Great," I grunt.

"Hey, let him go, Fred?" Gilda says. "He's my cousin?"

Fred squeezes tighter. "That true?"

"Yeah," I grunt. "Will you let go, or what?"

"Or what," he says, gripping harder.

I am trying to decide whether I should use my

elbows or my legs or my medical insurance when I hear Greb say "Down, boy. You got the picture. Come on. Let him go."

The next thing I know, I am crumpled in a heap on the concrete. I look up at Greb and a large neckless monster. They look down at me and smile. "Fred Pahinui," the monster says, extending a hand. "Pleased to meet you."

I look at the hand suspiciously. I have the feeling he may pull one of those ultra-squeeze handshakes on me. But no, he helps me up, almost gently. "Sorry," he apologizes. "I'm harmless."

"Unless you cross him," Greb notes.

"Just like to know what I'm up against," Fred says.

"Hey, man, the pamphlet?" Greb asks. "What do you think?"

"I was in the middle of reading it when some idiot came up and jumped me."

"Sorry," Fred mutters sheepishly.

"What do *you* think, if I can use the word 'think' around Greb?" Gilda asks Fred.

But of course Fred doesn't get a chance to answer, because Greb makes the thumbs-up sign and starts shouting. "It's gonna be *groove city!* STONE DREAD HIGH! BEYOND DREAD HIGH! BEYOND BAD HIGH! PUTRESCENT HIGH!"

We're all looking at Greb as if he's about to foam at the mouth or something, but there's no stopping him once he's on a roll. *"Not even just WARTY high! PUSTULANT high! RED high. HOT high. INFLAMED high. FESTERING OOZING high! Rah, rah, WARTY DUDES! YEAAAAAAA-AAH VOLCANOES!"*

"Greb, you've been overdosing on MTV again," Fred says quietly.

Greb comes down as fast as he went up. He looks at his watch. "Hey, got a job to do. I'm telling you — festering! Festering High! Yeah!" He makes the thumbs-up sign, thrusts his fist in the air, and disappears. We aren't exactly unhappy to see him go.

"So what do you think?" Fred asks.

I look at the next page:

THINGS TO BRING TO CARMODY HIGH:

> Pen
> Pencil
> Eraser
> Notebook
> Combination lock
> Gym shoes
> Brains
> Optional extras:
> > Whoopee cushion
> > Nose glasses
> > Wax lips
> > Pimples

"Weird," I say. "Weird."

"Come on, Ivan," Gilda whines. "Admit it. This is going to be great."

"It does sound slightly cooler than a regular high school," I admit. But then, what do I know?

I have never gone to high school before, and neither has Gilda. Maybe they're all like this.

But somehow I doubt it. I take another look at the picture on the front page. A bunch of those people in the costumes have fingers up their false noses.

I have never gone to high school before, and
neither has Dilda. Maybe they're all like this.
But somehow I doubt it. I only snatched a look
at the picture on the front page. A bunch of
white people in the nineties have funnier hair than Jake Rose.

NINE

Pustulous, as Greb would say. Festering. At ten the next morning I am staring at a familiar phrase. You know the one: **DO NOT OPEN THIS BOOK UNTIL YOU ARE TOLD TO DO SO.**

Right. An official test. Everybody has already taken it, except for me, so I can't even talk to the guidance counselor until I get this thing done. And since the high school offices aren't finished yet, I have to take it at a try-and-squash-in desk here at the primary school, where this first-grade classroom is the only one they've got a key for.

Some cute first grader must have stashed a carton of chocolate milk in the first desk I try. The reason I know this is that I now have chocolate milk all over my new shorts. You can hardly notice the brown stain against the neon green — if you're blind. Festering, all right.

DO NOT OPEN THIS BOOK UNTIL YOU ARE TOLD TO DO SO. Naturally, I lift up the corner and peek. I don't see anything, but at least it relieves the tension. And I know I can get away with it, because this hatchet-faced old crank named Ms. Rudge is staring at her watch at the front desk. They obviously did not name Comedy High after her. She is some sort of assistant vice-principal and she is supposed to time this test, and she can't quite figure out how to work this crummy little digital stopwatch. Every time she presses one of the buttons on the side, it beeps at her. From the faces she makes, you'd think it was farting.

Rudge sticks her head out of the room and hollers somebody's name. An old guy comes to the door and shows her what to do. Except he can't get the watch to work either. I put my hand up and shout, "Excuse me?"

Rudge gives me one of those classic teacher looks and says, "You'll just have to be patient."

"I know how to work those watches," I tell her.

Rudge and her henchman stare at me from the hall and look at each other suspiciously. They mumble to each other so I can't hear, but I don't have to hear to know what they're thinking. They're thinking I'll cheat somehow, give myself extra time or something. What this says about what they think of the student body is not exactly a good omen.

"I do," I say. "I used to have one." I don't bother to mention that it croaked.

Rudge crooks her finger at me, meaning I should get up and go over to where they are standing. No way is she going to walk twenty feet to me. So I pry myself out of the dumb little first-grade desk and go over and take the watch from her hands.

"An hour, right?"

Rudge nods and makes a constipated face. I play around with the little buttons until we're in stopwatch mode and the display says 1:00:00. "Just press the top button when it's time to start," I say. "It'll count down."

Does she say "Thank you?" Three guesses. What does she say? If your guess is "Take your seat," you get to go on to the jackpot round.

I sit down. So does Rudge. "There are no right answers," she reads aloud. "There are no wrong answers. You are not going to be graded. But you must answer every question. If you can't decide on an answer, make your best guess. You'll have one hour to finish, which should be more than enough time. Any questions?"

I put my hand up. Rudge gives me this sour look. "What?"

"How can there be no right or wrong answers?"

"This is not a test of factual knowledge."

"I don't get it. What's the point?"

"It is used for evaluation," she says. "Every entering sophomore has already taken it. Don't worry. It's not going to bite you."

That's the kind of thing people say when something's going to stab you or stomp you to a bloody pulp.

"Are you ready?"

Why not? If it weren't for this cramped chair, I wouldn't mind a bit. I love taking tests. I'm good at it. And I can see from the score sheet peeking out of the book that this one's multiple guess — my favorite. The big trick is to work backward when you're not sure what they're getting at.

"You have one hour," says Rudge. "You may open the book." She presses a button on the watch. It beeps at her. She looks surprised.

"Don't worry," I tell her as I open the book. "It's supposed to do that."

"Silence, please," says Rudge. Well, at least she knows the word "please."

First question:

1. You've got a choice of five TV shows. You watch:

    A. Shakespeare's *Hamlet*.
    B. Monday Night Football.
    C. Live from the Comedy Center.
    D. National Business News.
    E. Gambling for Fun and Profit.

"Weird!" I say to myself. "Weird!"

Except I guess I didn't say it quite to myself, because Rudge barks, "No talking! And be sure to make your marks good and dark."

I stare at the question. What would I do? In real life I would flip through the channels with my remote control and watch about twenty shows at once.

"And stay inside the lines," Rudge reminds me.

So, okay. I fill in Box C on the scoring sheet. Then I fill in A, B, D, and E. Next question.

2. Your friend slips and falls while you're playing touch football. You:

    A. Run to find the vice-principal for help.

    B. Bet your friend won't get up again.

    C. Get annoyed because your friend messed up the play.

    D. Imitate your friend by falling yourself.

    E. Laugh at your friend's clumsiness.

Where's "F. It all depends?" I mean, sure, you might laugh. Anyway, I might laugh. If it was one of those days when you were in kind of a silly mood, and if the fall looked really goofy, you might imitate it, particularly if the guy who falls isn't somebody who could beat you up. If he's a real jerk, you might say "Bet he won't get up again!" And if it's a big game against somebody you're really trying to beat, you might get annoyed.

I fill in all the answers but A. Our assistant principal back home was so lame he walked around with masking tape on his glasses. Some help he'd be! And Rudge here — well, forget it!

Then I erase C. The only way I'd get into a game where anything counted is if the whole team fell down.

And suddenly I realize something's fishy. This test is too weird. There's more going on here than meets the eye. Let's see:

3. When I hear the expression "1 2 3,"
   I think of:

   A. A time of day.
   B. A baseball score.
   C. The odds on a bet.
   D. A dance step.
   E. A person with a dental problem.

"One two three. One two three." I'm trying to think of what I think of when I see the expression "One two three." The dance step is the only one that makes sense.

Then I notice it says "*hear* the expression," not "*see* the expression." It's noticing details like this that makes me such a great test-taker. I say it under my breath. "One two three. One two three."

Okay. I get it. It's not just "one two three." It could also be "one to three." So it could be the time of day or the odds on a bet. It couldn't be a baseball score, because in baseball, you always give the leading team's score first, so it would be "three to one." But maybe whoever wrote the test didn't know that. Rudge doesn't exactly look like a baseball fan.

That's four out of five. But I can't even imagine why anyone in his right mind would think of a person with a dental problem.

So I try a little test psychology. I try to figure out why anybody wants to know what I think of when I hear the expression "One two three."

"One two three," I say under my breath again. "One . . . to three. Onetothree."

"No talking," Rudge says again, looking over

the top of some paperback mystery with a picture of a bloody dagger on the cover.

"Onetoothree," I say in my head. And then I get it! The person with the dental problem! One-tooth Ree! Got it!

One-tooth Ree! Corny or what? But I've got it, all right: I've got it all! I've got the whole deal, the answer to my question about what the test is for. In fact, I'm kind of annoyed at myself for taking this long to get it. What Rudge is keeping locked up in her sour little head is that this is what they're going to use to place me in one of the five "colleges."

Five "colleges": Five choices per question. Add 'em up, and they figure out where you should be. Am I smart, or what? But now I have to decide where I *want* to be. Fast.

I rule out Sports instantly. I'm a great baseball fan, but as a player I always get picked dead last. I hate football and don't care about basketball. Ten-year-olds can wipe me off the tennis court. The sports I really enjoy are hiking and cross-country skiing, and somehow I don't think we're likely to field a competitive team.

Hospitality? Dad and I are lousy cooks, and we don't clean our apartment until it's totally gross. I'd probably flunk Bedmaking 101, not to mention Advanced Bathroom Maintenance.

Performing and Comedy wouldn't be too bad, except for one major problem: I have a father who has proved how hard it is to make a living in the performing arts. Call me a wimp, but somehow I like the idea of a steady job.

This leaves Wagering. Too bad they don't have a College of Science Arts and Sciences, which is what I'd pick if they did. But I'm good at math. I like it. Figuring odds and stuff might help in some future scientific career that didn't happen to involve rolling dice or dealing cards.

"Zellner, are you daydreaming?" Rudge snatches my scoresheet into her gnarled hand. "You filled in all the blanks to question one."

"I thought there were no wrong answers."

"There are no wrong answers. But you get only one per question." She hands back the scoresheet.

"So-o-o-o sorry." I say, flipping my pencil over.

"Be sure you erase cleanly," says Rudge.

What I would love to erase is that sour expression from her face. But now that I know my goal, I'm going to have to erase anyway.

The theme is gambling, betting, and odds. For question 1, the answer is E: Gambling for Fun and Profit. For question 2, it's B: Bet your friend won't get up again. 3? You guessed it.

The rest of the test? Easiest I've ever taken. I'm done with twenty minutes to spare. When I hand in my paper, Rudge stares at her watch and looks at me as though she can't believe it. "You answered every question?"

"Yup."

"You've still got twenty minutes. Do you want to take time to check your answers?"

"Already did. Besides, there are no wrong answers — right?"

Rudge looks disappointed. "Take your seat.

91

Your appointment with the vice-principal isn't for another twenty-five minutes. Your parents won't be here till then."

"Parent," I say.

Rudge squinches up her face.

"What am I supposed to do?" I ask.

Rudge gives me this couldn't-care-less shrug.

"Can I borrow a newspaper or something? There's nothing to read in here except stuff for little kids."

"Surely you can find something to do."

I point. "TV?"

"You know how to operate it?"

"I'm even better with TVs than I am with watches."

Rudge gives me a deep sigh. "All right. Just don't play it too loud."

I turn the TV on. "This has been another edition of Classroom Satellite News — making students better citizens."

An enormous guy with eighty-eight chins and a string tie suddenly fills the screen. "Remember, kids," he says, "this fine programming has been brought to you by Pork Power, the deep-fried pork rinds that are the snack food part of every nutritious diet. They're the choice of presidents, future presidents — and smart kids like you. Mmmm-hmmm crunchy: That's Jeeter's Pork Power!"

Yeah. It's Jeeter P. Carmody. He's into food as good for the body as his casinos are for the soul. What I can't figure out is why our new high school doesn't have a college of Snack Food Technology.

* * *

Twenty minutes later my Dad and I are in the counselor's office.

"Interesting results on our entrance evaluation test, Mr. Zellner," says Mr. Seacrist, who resembles a weasel with a tiny moustache. "We believe your son cheated."

Dad gives me this look of amazement. I mean, I never cheat. Don't want to. Don't need to. Dad knows it.

"Cheated?" I say. "How could I cheat? Nobody was in the room with me. And there aren't supposed to be any right or wrong answers."

"Nevertheless," says Seacrist. This is the first time I have ever heard that used as an entire sentence.

"Nevertheless what?" Dad asks.

"Your son's answers are outside the normal variation. Well outside."

"What is the problem here?" Dad says impatiently. "Did he cheat or didn't he?"

"The test asked for honest answers to the questions. We believe" — he glances at the scoresheet to remind himself of my name — "Ivan answered the questions in such a way as to influence the results in the direction he was seeking."

Dad turns to me. "Well, did you?"

I squirm. "Maybe a little."

"A little?" says Seacrist. "Every single answer on this form points to the same conclusion. Every single answer points to an interest in gambling or betting. Not one answer suggests anything else."

Well, that's a relief, I think to myself. At least I didn't screw up. At least I got a hundred. My test-taking skills are still intact.

Seacrist rumbles on. "I find it impossible to believe you can be that obsessed with the subject."

"How much you want to bet?" I shoot back.

"Very funny," says Seacrist, and I can see Dad agrees, because he's biting his lip to keep from cracking up. "Further evidence of your true aptitude."

"What's that?" Dad asks in a slightly giddy tone.

"We are going to place Ivan in the College of Comedic Arts."

Dad shoots him a major frown. "Mr. Seacrist, I'm a professional musician. Occasionally I get paid to do what I love. But most of the time I get paid to do what I dislike or hate, and sometimes I don't get paid at all. I am not going to encourage my only son to take up any kind of performing. It's a lousy life."

"I'm sorry you feel that way," Seacrist says. "But unfortunately Comedy is the only College where we have room at the moment."

"Wait a minute!" I shriek. "Why did I take the test?"

"Regulations. Procedures." Seacrist cracks a smile. "And we do have to keep Ms. Rudge busy."

"Nice going," Dad says as we walk out the door and into the heat. "Outsmarted yourself."

"I'm not a cheater. Guess I should've messed up a couple of questions to throw them off the trail, huh?"

Dad nods.

"Hey, look on the bright side," I tell him. "At least I've got Greb to keep me company."

Dad makes a face. "As far as I'm concerned that's not a bright side."

"Maybe comedy will actually come in handy," I say.

Dad makes an uglier face.

"Lots of money in comedy," I say. "Lots of jobs."

"Like what?"

I think about it. "Comedian. Comic. Comic-book artist. Cartoonist. Comedy writer. Comedy club owner. Comedy club manager. Comedy club waiter. Clown. Court jester?"

"Court jester!"

"You never know when royalty may come back. Okay, comedy . . . you made me lose my train of thought . . . comedy . . . comedy . . . doctor. Comedy lawyer. Comedy plumber."

"Yeah, right," Dad mutters. "Or comedy Senator. Comedy President of the United States. There've been a lot of clowns in those jobs."

"See?" I say. "What did I tell you?"

TEN

It's a two-test day. I need a job, the casinos need warm bodies, and in this weather, my body is as warm as it gets. I take up Caitlin's suggestion and head for the Silver Bullet. Dad says to ask for Personnel, but the Silver Bullet doesn't have a personnel department. They have what they call Central Casting.

The application form explains that the Silver Bullet doesn't hire people. It "casts" them as "part of the wonderful western movie that we create each day for our honored guests." I guess that's one way to look at it.

I remember what Caitlin told me about the Bounty Hunt, so I make sure I put her name where it asks who recommended me. It takes a couple of seconds until I remember her last name.

When I flip the form over, I find this little test. There are supposed to be no right answers on this one, either. Ha!

It doesn't matter. I've got this one nailed, too. They ask you things like "I tell a lie . . ."

A. Never
B. Rarely
C. Occasionally
D. Often

Well, you know that nobody in the world has *never* told a lie, so if you answer "Never," they'll figure you are the kind of person who lies to make yourself look good. If you say you lie a lot, they may figure you'll steal the silverware or something. Correct answer: B.

When I'm all done, Mr. Casting — actually, his badge says *Bob* and *Ohio* — stares at me and asks, "So you think it's okay to lie once in a while?"

"Well, sometimes, if it's not something important and you don't want to hurt somebody's feelings."

Right answer. Right lie. Bob smiles and takes a puff on his cigarette. He pushes a few keys on his computer. "You ever dip ice cream?"

"Sure. At home." I mean, I don't stick my face in the carton, do I?

"I think we'll start you at Western Scoop," he says. "Frozen Dessert Specialist. Do well, and there's no telling how high you can go."

"Gee, great," I exclaim, though I don't exactly imagine they're going to promote me to his job anytime soon.

"Remember, your goal is to make our guests happy at all times." He hands me a little pamphlet. "Here are our corporate regulations. Be clean, neat, friendly, and on time, and you'll go far here at the Silver Bullet." He puts his cigarette in an ashtray, stands up, and extends his hand. We shake.

"Thanks," I say, though I don't add, "for making my hand smell like a cigarette."

"Don't mention it. When can you start?"

"Right now."

"Fine." He hands me a little slip of paper. "Take this down to the Green Room. Level B."

Caitlin was right. Half an hour and I've got a job. Just like that. Not bad.

When I get off the cast-only elevator at level B, a couple of women speaking Spanish are waiting to push their cleaning carts on. Their maid uniforms have embroidered curlicues and pearl buttons on the front. Everybody's part of the wonderful western movie.

I find the Green Room. A large black woman in normal human clothes is sitting at a desk at the entrance. Her badge says *Betty* and *Chicago*. She takes the slip of paper from my hand, then lifts up her glasses and squints at it. "Lord, that guy has bad handwriting. You know what this says?"

I take a look. It's just a mess of scribble, but finally I scope it out. "Western Scoop?"

She gives me this tired sigh. "Oh, yeah." She looks me up and down and presses a few keys on her keyboard.

"You know your waist size?"

"Twenty-eight?"

She reaches into her desk and tosses me a tape measure. "Let's make sure."

I put the tape measure around my waist. She pulls it taut, grabs it back, and pushes a couple of keys. She looks me up and down. "Okay. Wait here."

I stand there. A bunch of cowgirl maids pass by, giggling in some Asian language. Betty from Chicago returns with two coat hangers with two black plastic bags over them. In her other hand is a huge cowboy hat.

"Let's try this for fit." She pounds the hat on my head, and stands back to inspect me. She turns her head one way and then the other. "It'll do."

A woman goes by in one of those barely-there dancehall-hostess outfits. I swivel my head for a look. "Hey, honey, you get all distracted, you won't last long on the job," says Betty, handing me the clothes and a little piece of paper. "Take this stuff back to the men's locker room and put it on. That's your locker number and combination. Keep it with you, and don't leave your money or anything valuable in there."

The men's locker room is about what you'd find in a gym, only smaller. Nobody's there except a guy who's adjusting his string tie in a mirror. "First job here?" he asks without turning around.

"Yeah," I say, fiddling with my combination.

"Don't let 'em screw you." He turns around, makes a gun with his thumb and forefinger, shoots me and leaves. "Good luck!"

I get undressed and take the outfit out of the

bag. I'm a cowboy, all right, right down to the holster. I take the hat off, put the rest of the stuff on, and check the mirror. Not bad. I slam on the hat. Not bad at all. I look totally cool — for 1875. I'm Ivan the Kid. "You're one tough hombre," I say to my image.

"You look about as tough as a slice of Wonder bread." In the mirror I can see behind me an enormous shoulder and, above that, a black sombrero with a bunch of dangling tassels.

I turn around. It's Fred Pahinui. "You look about as Mexican as Emperor Hirohito," I tell him.

Fred looks slightly hurt. "Hey, man, I'm not Japanese. I'm Hawaiian. And Samoan." I notice his badge says *Fred* and *Hilo*.

"No offense. Sorry. What kind of job do you do in that outfit?"

"Tee-Sass."

"Huh?"

"T-S-A-S. Tortilla, Salsa, and Agua Specialist."

"One more time?"

"Hey, I'm a busboy in the Mexican restaurant. But they can't just say that. Everybody gets a phony name here. Everybody's a 'specialist.' It's supposed to make you proud of your job. What did they give you."

"Western Scoop?"

"Frozen Dessert Specialist! I used to do that before they decided I was eating too much of the stuff. Where's your mask?"

"My what?"

"Your mask!" He grabs something from a coat hanger and tosses it at me. "Here you go, champ."

100

It's a mask, all right. Fred grabs my hat and holds it above my head. I put the mask on. He slams the hat down on my noggin. After I recover from whiplash, I stare at myself in the mirror. "I either look tough, or as stupid as any human being on the face of the earth."

"You said it, man, I didn't. Hey, you better get up there. They dock you for lateness."

"Not good for the wonderful western movie, right?"

"Right. Hey, wait! You can't go up there like that."

"Like what?"

He points to my feet. "Sneakers?"

"Zellner, you in there?" shouts Betty's voice from the hall.

"Yeah!" I shout back.

Two western boots fly through the door. "Put these on and get moving!" she hollers. "You got about five minutes to get upstairs."

"What did I tell you?" asks Fred Pahinui.

I put on the boots. They're kind of tight, but I guess they'll do for now. I lock up my locker.

"Watch," says Pahinui.

"Watch what?"

He points to his wrist. "Take off your watch. They didn't have digital in pioneer days. Wrist either."

I take off the watch and stick it in my pocket. I head back to the front desk. Chicago Betty pushes a piece of paper in front of me. "Sign here."

The paper says I am responsible for all damage to my costumes except for normal wear and tear.

If I don't return them in good condition at the end of my term of employment, I will pay the sum of $500.

"Five hundred dollars!" I exclaim.

"That's for two of them. We clean them twice a week. These getups are custom-made. We want you to take care of them."

"What if I get ice cream on them or something?"

"No problem. That's normal wear and tear. And remember, they don't leave the premises — not even on Halloween. We want 'em back."

I give her a dirty look as I sign the page.

"Good luck, pardner." Betty hands me a badge that says, *Ivan* and *Seatle*.

"Seattle is misspelled here," I point out.

"I thought it looked kind of funny," Betty says. "We'll send up a new one as soon as we can. Meanwhile, Level 2, turn left. Ask for Sam."

I step off the cast-only elevator at level 2. The Western Scoop sign is just across the hall. A darkskinned guy in an Indian costume and thick glasses is dipping a cone for a fat little girl and her fatter mom. The girl is singing "chocolate, chocolate, chocolate," over and over again.

"You got it," says the ice-cream Indian. He leans over the counter and hands her the cone.

The little girl takes a lick. "This isn't chocolate!"

"Oh, it's chocolate, all right," says the guy in the Indian costume. "Chocolate, chocolate, chocolate."

"Isn't!"

"Is!" says the Indian.

"Honey, it really is chocolate," says the girl's mother. She takes a lick. "Mmmm. Good." She hands it back to her daughter.

"*You* have it. I want chocolate."

"I'm sorry," says the mother, handing it back to the guy in the Indian costume. "I guess she's kind of confused. I'd eat it myself, but I'm on a diet."

The Indian smiles. "No problem. Good luck!" He stands there holding the cone.

"It's okay, honey," the woman tells her daughter. "If you want chocolate, we'll find you chocolate."

"Yes!" says the girl. She sticks her tongue out at the Indian as she walks away.

"You must be the new guy," the Indian says to me, tossing the cone into a big waste can behind the counter. "I'm out of arrows, so would you shoot those people for me? Plain lead bullet, please. A silver bullet is too good for them."

I laugh and check his badge. *Sam. Los Angeles.* "I guess you're the Sam I'm supposed to ask for."

He bows from the waist. "Sami Chandresekar. At your service."

"Any relation to the famous astronomer?"

Sam looks amazed. "You know about him!"

"I'm interested in astronomy."

"Not me. My parents say we're not related anyhow."

"Indian name, right?"

Sam nods. "Indian Indian. Not American Indian. Ironic, huh? That guy in Casting thinks he has a great sense of humor."

"I'd be surprised if he thinks at all."

"If only Christopher Columbus could see this, huh?"

"Or General Custer," I say.

"You mean 'General Custard,' pard," says Sam. "One of our many superbly delicious frozen dessert specialties."

I notice somebody familiar stroll by in a well-filled cowgirl costume. "Hey, Caitlin!" I holler. "Cait!"

She stops in her tracks and looks my way. She obviously doesn't recognize me in this outfit. I lift my mask and wave at her.

"What'syourname!" She comes over to the counter. "You're the guy who was with His Wartiness yesterday!"

I put back the mask. "The name's Ivan the Kid. Thanks for the tip about the job."

"No big deal. Hey, did you remember to put me down for the Bounty Hunt?"

"No. I just put down 'what'shername.' "

Caitlin stands there and stares at me. "You didn't!"

"Hey, you didn't remember *my* name."

"Aw, come on, Ivan. Wait a minute! You just called my name. You're putting me on, right?"

I shrug and tip my hat. "Could be, Miz McKibbin."

Caitlin smiles, relieved. "Just remember, you've got to stay on for a month, or I don't get my bonus. And you're already falling down on the job."

"Huh?" I wonder if my pants are slipping.

"You're supposed to have ice-cream scoops in those holsters."

"Really?" I ask Sam.

He nods, half-embarrassed. "Hey, I don't think these things up."

"What time you get off work, Ivan the Kid?" Caitlin asks.

"Nine."

"Me too. You live in Carmody?"

"Where else is there?"

"Well, Finger?"

I respond with the official one-digit response.

"Greb has taught you well, I see," she says. "That does mean you live this side of the river?"

"Correct," I reply.

"You need a ride home?"

"Why not?"

"Hey, what about me?" Sam says. "I live here, too."

"You're a supervisor," Caitlin points out. "You're stuck here till ten."

And I think, well, maybe there are good things about starting at the bottom.

ELEVEN

Now I know why the high school doesn't have a College of Snack Food Technology. *This* is the College of Snack Food Technology.

Sam is a pretty good teacher. I learn how to dip ice cream without breaking the cones. I learn how to dip ice cream so that the customer thinks there's more than there actually is. I learn how to always ask "a double?" to make the suckers feel cheap and hungry so maybe they'll spend more. I learn how to run the cash register. I learn how to make a couple of Western Scoop specials, including the Sidewinder Sundae and the Apache Shake. I learn how to take the scoops out of my holsters and twirl them. I learn how to wash them off when I miss and they fall to the floor.

I also learn that our customers are mostly kids

on vacation with their parents, and they're either so little they show up with their parents or they're bored out of their skulls because their parents are downstairs in the part of the casino where they're not allowed to go. Girls even come up to flirt with us, but they all seem to be about nine years old. "We're approved flirtation devices," Sam says.

The line we hear most from kids our own age is, "Is there anything to do around here?" We point them to the video arcade, but they've already been to the video arcade. We tell them about the swimming pool, but they're already sick of the swimming pool. We tell them how to get to the bowling alley up at Jeeter P.'s Carmody Inn, and they make faces at us because their parents have told them not to leave the hotel. When we ask if they want to buy ice cream, they kind of slouch away. Sam says it's probably because they pigged out at our all-you-can-eat buffet.

I'm so busy learning stuff that I don't have a chance to think about Caitlin until the end of my shift. What makes me remember is an unmistakable voice behind me as I clean the counter. "Warty! Far out! It's the official beginning of the most pustulous Labor Day Weekend ever! Yes!"

Guess who. And normally I wouldn't mind seeing him. Under the circumstances, I'm not exactly thrilled.

"Hey, man, you ready?" Greb says.

"You've been here for two days so far and you already know this guy?" Sam asks me.

"Hey, we're buddies to the max," Greb says.

"He's a local institution," Sam tells me. "He should be *in* a local institution."

"Ignore this guy, man," Greb says. "Totally uncool. Mr. Luke Warm. Sam Old Thing."

"Hey, Sam's okay."

"Hey, I understand, man. Say nice things about the boss. No problem.

"Why shouldn't he?" Sam says matter-of-factly. "His boss is a great guy." Actually, Sam is cool, in a kind of dry, quiet way.

"So what time you get off?" Greb asks me.

I think about that test question about how often I tell lies. But I just can't do it. "Nine."

"Great! You know about the clocks, right?"

"Yeah, I told him," Sam says.

The rule is that there are no clocks visible anywhere in the hotels and casinos. The idea is that if you can't see a clock, you might gamble longer. The way they stack the odds, the longer they keep you gambling, the more money you're likely to lose.

Greb points to his watch. "You're free, pardner."

"Uh, not exactly." I start to take off my apron. "It's okay, right, Sam?"

"Yeah. Nice job. You have a real future in the frozen dessert business."

In one swift motion, I twirl my ice cream scoops at him and dump them in the sink.

"Hey, this is the official start of the beginning of the end. Our last three days of freedom before Festering High!"

Why is it that Greb is beginning to get on my

108

nerves? Actually, I can think of a couple of reasons.

"I've kind of got a date," I say quietly as I walk around the counter.

"Fast worker! Who?"

"Caitlin."

"Caitlin? No kidding?"

"Well, sort of," I say. "I mean, she's driving me home."

"Great! She can drive us both."

"Greb, this is the two of us."

"You and me."

"Me and her."

"Oh, come on. Save me a buck."

"Hey, that reminds me. You owe me two from the other day."

"Man, did I charge you for the wartiest tour in town?"

I don't want to seem cheap, but the way things have been with Dad, two bucks is a major portion of my financial empire, and who knows what might happen tonight? I give Greb my patented "shame on you" look.

"All right, all right." He digs into his pocket and takes out two sick-looking bills. He uncrumples them to make sure they're singles. He hands them to me. "Here, your pustulence."

I keep the bills in my hand so I won't leave them in the costume. "Don't mention it, your flatulence."

Caitlin comes up behind us. "Your flatulence! Hey, I like that. Perfect name for this gasbag."

Greb burps.

"Thank you, Greb," Caitlin says with a little bow.

"Anytime," he belches.

"You still want that ride?" Caitlin asks me.

"You bet." I give Greb this look that says please don't put your two cents worth in. I am totally amazed when he doesn't.

"Well, we've both got to change, so let's hit the 'vator." Caitlin says. We head down the hall.

"See you, Greb!" I shout over my shoulder. He responds with another belch. I feel slightly rotten about leaving him there, but then he and I didn't really have anything planned, and Caitlin and I sort of do.

"So what do you think?" she asks me.

"I feel like an old cowhand," I drawl.

She rolls her eyes. "Some old lady bought ten key chains that have dice and the words *Carmody, Future Entertainment Capital of the World* on them. She's sending them to all her grandchildren. Imagine how thrilled they're going to be."

"Yeah," I say. "Think of the thank-you notes their parents will make them write."

She presses the *Down* button. The door opens and a bald, beefy security guy is standing there. As we move past him, Caitlin whispers, "His fly's open."

We crack up. The bald guy turns around and gives us the dirty look adults give you when they know you're making fun of them. Unfortunately, he doesn't turn around far enough for me to check whether his fly really is open.

When the door is about one inch from fully closed, we hear a familiar voice yelling, "Hey, guys, wait up!" Before we can react, the bald guy leans on the *Close Door* button.

"Thanks, mister!" we say at the same time, and start giggling again. The bald guy scowls at us as he gets off on the ground floor.

"Meet out here in five?" Caitlin asks me as we reach the green room door. There's an old guy at the front desk now. He's wearing a uniform and what looks like a real gun. He's also smoking. This town must have a tobacco plantation in it somewhere.

"Make it ten," I say. "It may take me that long to hang up all this crap."

In the locker room, a couple of dealers in those string ties wave hello with their cigarettes and then go back to talking. I wave back and change into my street clothes. I check the mirror. The hat has messed up my hair, but I don't have my hairbrush with me, or even a comb. I smooth it down the best I can and head for the hallway.

Caitlin is waiting out there. She looks different somehow — less like an adult, more like a kid. I mean, in the cowgirl outfit she could've passed for twenty-one. Well, maybe nineteen. Now she looks my age and kind of plain, except for that chest of hers. She's probably thinking the same thing about me, not counting my chest.

"Radical clash!" she says as I approach. "We can't both be allowed to live!" What she means is her pink neon shorts and my green neon shorts are pretty awful together.

She tugs at the sleeve of my T-shirt. "Sniff," she says.

I do. "Yuck. Smells like a smoked skunk."

"Everything around here gets that way. Next time bring a plastic bag and stick your clothes in it. It helps a little. But you still get the smell in your hair and stuff. When you work around here, you get used to taking a lot of showers."

"The smelly ones we're not supposed to take because of the drought?"

"You got it."

"Could you tell me one thing? How come everybody smokes around here?"

"Haven't you figured it out yet? This town is about losing. People come here to win, but most of them don't. They can't. Losing is what keeps this town in business. And who smokes?"

"Losers," I guess.

"You win," Caitlin says.

We go outside to the employee parking lot. The air has cooled off a little, but it stinks from the power plant. I hold my nose.

"It usually smells worse at night," Caitlin says. "Get used to it. We're a twenty-four hour town. We keep the lights burning all night. We've got air-conditioning so nobody needs to stay out in the stink." She stops in front of a big old Mercury and takes out her keys.

"This is yours?"

"Sure is," Caitlin says proudly. "The Incredible Hulk."

It's a hulk, all right. A real beater. The paint is flaking off, and stuffing is coming out of the seats, and you have to work the door handle just right or it falls off. Inside, the car is still warm. But it starts right up, and the air-conditioning comes on full blast in a couple of seconds.

"Bet you didn't think it would start," Caitlin says.

"I had some doubts."

"I have to let it warm up a second, or it'll stall out."

"Still, not bad."

"Did you eat yet?" she asks.

"My practice Sidewinder Sundae?"

"God, if I had your job, I'd weigh five hundred pounds and be a giant human zit. You want to get some real food?"

"One of the buffets?"

"You kidding?" She turns to me. "I used to have this weight problem? I finally figured out it was from the buffets every night?"

"Every night?"

"Five out of seven, anyway. My mom gets a free meal. It was easier to bring me along than cook for me."

"Did she blimp up?"

"You kidding? She loves buffets. Knows how to handle them. Eats the salads and maybe a slice of bread, and nobody can say she ought to eat more. She has to watch her figure like a hawk. Her job and all."

"What kind of job?'

"Nude dancer," she says, as though she's challenging me to make something of it. "Anyway, as nude as it gets around here."

"Greb's mom does that, too," I say.

"Greb's mom? Who told you that?"

"His flatulence."

"Dirk *wishes* his mom did that," Caitlin says. "Did you ever *see* his mom?"

"No," I admit.

"She's as fat as Greb is skinny. Mostly she hangs around casino bars and drinks. When she's not gambling."

"You're kidding. Does she work?"

"Last I heard, she was a slot machine technician. You know, collects money from them. Fixes them. Hey, don't tell him I told you about the drinking stuff. He's kind of weird about it."

"I guess so."

"Hey, meanwhile, I'm starved. And if we sit here much longer with the motor running, we're potential candidates for carbon monoxide poisoning."

I get a bright idea. "Pizza? My dad said he found an okay place over in Finger City."

"I know the place." Caitlin smiles and shakes her head. "But you are from another planet. Finger's Arizona."

"I didn't say it was Italy."

Caitlin gives me this exasperated look. "I'm not that great a driver yet. And there are a lot more cops that side of the river, and they're a lot tougher than they are over here. Traffic tickets are a big business in Finger, and when you're our age, they can screw up your insurance. I mean, I like pizza, but I'm not going to sacrifice my whole driving career for it."

"What about this side?"

"Only place in Carmody is Petra's. We call it Putrid's. Their pizza tastes about as good as the town smells."

"Hey, I know," I say. "My dad just bought a

whole mess of frozen pizzas over at Price Cutter. You can come over to our place."

As soon as I get the words out, I realize that this is the first time I have ever invited a girl to come to my house for dinner alone. Well, hey, Carmody is supposed to be different. "The place is a little messy, though. Just moving in and everything."

"Is your dad home?" Caitlin asks suspiciously.

"Not for a couple of hours."

Caitlin leans over and gives me a quick peck on the cheek. "It's a deal."

TWELVE

Caitlin is, uh, an interesting driver. She's safe, doesn't push the speed limit or anything, but every time we start up from a stop, the car lurches forward.

"How long did you say you've been driving?" I ask, realizing the moment I say it that maybe I should have just shut up.

"Very funny," says Cait. "It's not me. It's the car. My mom's doesn't do this when I drive it."

"Then you should call this thing the bucking bronco."

"Hey! Don't you go insulting my baby!" She pats the dashboard lovingly. I should be so lucky.

"So-o-o-o . . ."

" . . . sorry!" we both say together, cracking up.

"Somebody told me it might be a transmission

problem," Caitlin says. "What do you think?"

"I don't. I don't know much about cars." No sense bringing up exactly how little I do know.

"What do you have?" Caitlin asks.

"I don't."

"You mean you're not sixteen yet?"

Caught! Found out! Once she finds out she's older than I am, she'll dump me. Unless . . . how often did I say I lie? Oh, why bother? "Soon."

"You had driver's ed yet?"

I shake my head.

"Hey, great! *I* can teach you."

I guess my face gives away what I think of that idea, because she says, "Just kidding."

We lurch into one of the visitors' spaces at my apartment complex. We get out of the car and head toward my place. There are still a few people hanging out down at the far end of the pool, but in the dark I can't see who.

"Hey, Ivan, is that you?" Gilda shouts.

I ignore her.

"Ivan! Over here!"

"Somebody's calling," Caitlin sings.

"Yeah. My brain-damaged cousin."

"Who's that?"

"Gilda."

"Gilda Dunkel?" Caitlin sneers.

"Don't hold it against me."

Then I hear not just one voice, but two, screaming at the top of their lungs. "*I-VAN!*"

"I'll wait here," says Caitlin, sitting down on the stairs.

"You two don't get along?" I ask.

"*I-VAN!*" Gilda screams even louder.

117

"Not exactly," Caitlin says.

I stroll down the pool. Gilda and Wendy pop up from the deep. "Something wrong with your hearing?" Gilda asks.

"It's that girl he's with. Got him all distracted." Wendy swims away.

"Yeah, I'll say. Who is that cow, Ivan?"

"She's not a cow," I say. "And she's none of your business. What do you want, anyway?"

"I'm supposed to tell you that we're leaving for the picnic at nine tomorrow."

"Huh?" I say.

"From my place? On the boat?"

Now I remember. There's supposed to be a picnic and boat ride with Gilda and Penny and Penny's boyfriend and Dad and who knows who else.

"Okay. I'll remember."

Wendy swims back. "You know who the cow is? Caitlin McKibbin, that's who."

"Yuck! Ivan, I thought you had some taste?" says Gilda.

"She's a cow, all right," says Wendy.

"Bull," I tell her.

"No," says Gilda. "Cow. C-o-w?"

"Very funny," I say. "What's supposed to be wrong with her?"

"Us to know and you to find out," Gilda sings.

"You're full of it." I walk away.

"Mooooo!" Gilda shouts, and then Wendy takes it up, too. "Mooooo!" The sound echoes in the courtyard. It sounds filthy, evil.

I give them a dirty look over my shoulder. "Great cousin you have there, Ivan," Cait says.

"You don't get to pick your relatives. Come on. Let's get something to eat."

As we climb the stairs we can still hear mooing and giggling from down below. "I'm half tempted to spit on them," Caitlin says. "Jerks." As we step through the door, she flips them the finger.

Inside, the rumble from the air conditioner blocks out the mooing. Caitlin takes a look around at all the boxes and junk. "Hey, nice place," she says, brushing a used sock from the couch.

"I warned you."

"Let's get going on that pizza. I'm starved."

Caitlin has a look around while I open the freezer and separate two pizzas that are stuck together. No problem. One of the great myths of TV comedy is that men have trouble cooking. As far as I'm concerned, cooking is just a matter of following directions. I read the instructions on the package, preheat the oven for 425°, and set the pizza on the counter.

I open the refrigerator door. "You want some pop?"

Caitlin comes over and takes out a diet root beer. I grab a Coke. "You got any chips or anything?"

"Probably. Depends what Dad stocked up on." I open a bunch of cabinets and find the tortilla chip stash.

"Nice going," says Caitlin. "I saw salsa in there." She dumps it in a bowl, and we head for the living room. We set the food down on a table Dad and I made from one of the moving cartons.

"I can't believe you're Gilda's cousin," Caitlin says. "God!"

"Hey, I don't like it any better than you do. Don't hold it against me."

"You don't know her. She's like the queen of the popularity parade."

"What do you mean?"

"I mean she's a bitch."

"Not exactly a lot upstairs either," I add. "And her friend Wendy's even lamer. Mostly I ignore them."

"Yeah, try. Good luck. You don't know how mean she can be if she wants to."

"What do you mean, I don't know? I just saw."

"I'm telling you, just watch out. She'll do things behind your back, and you won't even know what hit you."

"What did you ever do to her, anyway?"

"Me? I got these." With both hands, she points to her breasts. "I mean, it's not like I ordered them in a bigger size than hers. It's not like I flaunt them. They're what I've got. But Gilda's the queen. If you have something and she doesn't, she makes fun of you."

"It's not because you're black or anything?"

"You kidding? Ask anybody who's outside her little circle. She's an equal-opportunity bitch!"

I get up, grab the oven mitts, and turn myself into a boxer. "Fight back!"

"Forget it. Why stoop to her level?"

"I have to stoop to her level to get this pizza in the oven," I say, sliding it onto the rack. "Okay. Pepperoni liftoff in fifteen." Hmmm. Caitlin has disappeared.

"Hey, what is that big tubular thing in here?" she shouts from my bedroom.

I kind of blush. Number one, I didn't exactly expect Caitlin to take a tour of my bedroom while I was setting up the pizza. Number two, I immediately think of about seven dirty responses I would make if it were a guy who asked me that question.

I go into the bedroom and toss the underwear on my bed under the covers. "Part of my telescope."

"A real telescope? Like for astronomy?"

"Yeah."

"Can I look through it? I've never used a real telescope."

"Nothing to see yet. I haven't got it put together. Dad and I haven't had the time."

"Does your dad have to be here to do it?"

"No, I can. But you need two people."

"Well?" she says.

"Hey, great!"

"How long will it take?"

"Ten minutes? Fifteen?"

"Let's go."

I hunt up Dad's tool box. We take the telescope parts out and put them on my bed. As we're assembling the tripod, we begin to smell pizza. I look at my watch. "Food in five."

I tell Caitlin about all the neat stuff you can see through the telescope, and how it's even better if you can find a place away from the lights of the city. She says she knows a perfect spot on this side of the river, so we can drive there. We talk about this and that as we work on the tripod, and next thing we know, this incredibly loud horn noise blasts from the living room.

I run toward the kitchen. Smoke is pouring out of the oven. The pizza is a little, shall we say, overdone. "Well, at least your smoke detector works," says Caitlin, opening the windows. I grab a magazine and use it to blow air at the detector to get it to stop.

"Great," I say. "The one place in town without any smoke, and I go and crap it up."

We decide to get out of the place for awhile. We leave the windows open and head for Petra's Pizza. It's in this little shopping center next door to the gas station and pseudo-supermarket. There's hardly anybody in the place, but even so, nobody's in a hurry to take our order. Somebody finally shows up to write down medium pepperoni.

"Check those two out," says Caitlin, pointing to a couple of seedy-looking guys smoking and playing slot machines near the front door.

"They look like they've got a lot of luck. Get-rich-quick artists."

"Yeah," she snorts. "Stuck there. Like statues. When do you think they last changed their clothes. Or had a bath?"

"The way the air smells around here, who'd notice?"

"Gambling!" She laughs and shakes her head.

"Excuse me, but the term is 'gaming.' Or 'wagering.' Never call it gambling. It says so in the Silver Bullet cast handbook. I read it on my bathroom break."

"Right. They also call us 'cast' instead of employees. This whole town is built on lies," Caitlin says. "Like, which 'college' are you in?"

"For high school?"

"Yeah. Another lie. It's not exactly like we're getting college educations. Which one are you in?"

"What one do I look like?"

Caitlin thinks it over. "I give up."

"Comedy," I tell her. "I tried for Gaming, but they caught me cheating."

"Cheating?"

I explain it to her.

"Nice," she says. "If it makes you feel better, I *hate* sports."

"How did you wind up there?"

"Who knows?"

"Did you protest?"

"Sure. You know what they tell you? They tell you it doesn't matter for the first year anyhow, because the coursework is pretty much the same. Supposedly you'll be able to change at the end of the year. But what am I going to change to?"

"Not Comedy, huh?"

"I don't want somebody telling me how to tell jokes. I want somebody teaching me stuff I need to get into a good college. Somehow I don't think they're gonna look at your application and say 'Oh, great. This guy got straight A's in funny.' "

"Yeah, I know. Or terrific grades in soccer."

"Actually, the soccer might get you into college. Athletic scholarship. Weird. So my mom says to try my best. But I know I am going to be terrible."

"I know what you mean. I wanted to sign up for science stuff, but there isn't any. And the math is all gambling."

"Gaming," Caitlin corrects me.

"So-o-o-o sorry."

"Not bad. Maybe Comedy's the right place for you."

Somebody calls our number, and I go over to pick up our pizza. It's not burned, except for the edges, but Caitlin is right. It's a pretty sorry excuse for pizza.

"See," Caitlin says, "what I want is to get into law school or business school. What I don't want to do is end up where my mom is now. Dancing mostly naked in a dumb show? Barely making enough money to pay the rent? And what does she do when she loses her looks? Hey, no way."

"Same thing with my dad. He busts his butt for years studying music. He's great, but so what? What does he end up with? A lousy job playing for a lousy show."

"At least they're sort of doing what they like," Caitlin says through a mouthful of pizza.

"My dad? Are you kidding? He likes classical music. He hates this stupid show stuff. It's just the only job he could get, that's all."

"Well, my mom loves to dance. I mean, she's trained in classical ballet. She wanted to be on Broadway. Ended up here. Just goes to show you."

We eat our pizzas. We talk about life. By the time we're done, the only people in the place are the cashier and the two guys at the slot machines. "Maybe they've got the right idea," I say. "Strike it rich, forget about working."

"This town is lousy with people who had the right idea," Cait says. "They're all sitting in front

124

of slot machines waiting for their big jackpots to come in."

Caitlin drops me off at my place. As I get out of the car, she gives my cheek another quick peck.

"Was that a date?" I ask.

"Are you kidding?" Caitlin says, smiling. "That was a ride home. A date is when you give me a look through that telescope."

As she drives away, I can see the headline on the supermarket newspapers. **ASTRONOMY: HOT NEW TURN-ON.**

THIRTEEN

When I walk through the door, I can still smell
the pizza smoke. At least it's not cigarette smoke.

Dad is lying on the couch, reading a magazine
and sipping a beer. "I realize you're not exactly
fond of this place," he says without looking up,
"but burning it down may not be the best solu-
tion."

"Pizza accident. Sorry. In fact, so-o-o-o sorry."

Dad frowns at me over the top of his magazine.
"Cooking. It's all a matter of following directions." He has heard me say this about a million
times, so he is rubbing it in a little.

"Okay, okay. I get it. I get it."

"Maybe you can cook something for Penny's
picnic tomorrow. Something smoked, perhaps?"

"Do I have to go to that dorky picnic?"

"You and Gilda aren't exactly bosom buddies, are you?"

"Where'd you hear that?"

"Penny mentioned something about it."

"Gilda probably told her I'm a lame. And I feel the same way about her. Double. So do we have to go to this thing?"

"Family obligation, okay? Who knows? You might meet somebody interesting."

And I do. I meet Penny's boyfriend Zack. He's interesting, all right. He's a skinny guy with a leathery face and a screw-you attitude. He works in security at the Golden Spike, which is probably a good job for him. With his ten-gallon hat and silver belt buckle, he looks like a Western sheriff. Even talks like one. One false move and he'd probably shoot you between the eyes.

It's his boat that we're in, roaring up Lake Nevari toward the picnic spot. I am sitting back and enjoying the ride when Wendy and Gilda grab beers from the cooler. "Want one?" Gilda asks.

Innocent question? Ha! I don't even like beer. Too sour. No flavor. And it makes me nauseous. But if I say that, I can just see Gilda starting a rumor about how wimpy I am. If I just say no, I'm a dork. If I say yes, I'll probably get seasick all over the boat.

"Not right now," I say.

"Yeah. Right." Wendy sneers. "Maybe later, dude."

"Like in six years." Gilda hoots as though it's the funniest thing anybody's ever said. She and Wendy sit there drinking, thinking they look way cool, thinking I'm a dork. I can't figure out why I should care what they think, but I do, sort of.

There is not much to do on a boat. Gilda and Wendy are having an endless conversation about what they're going to wear for the first day of school. Dad is talking with Penny about where to shop in town. I go up front and ask Zack if I can steer.

"Sure thing, pard." He moves to let me into the captain's chair, keeping one hand on the wheel until I get there. "Just keep 'er steady. Aim about twenty feet to the left of that big rock."

"Got it."

"And take the big wakes crosswise."

"Right." I have driven my friends' parents' boats in Seattle. It's not exactly brain surgery.

"So what do you think of that jinxed high school of yours?"

"Jinxed?" I ask.

"Hoodooed. Bunch of ghosts still there from the big fire. No telling what they'll do when a bunch of kids disturb their rest."

I can't tell if he's serious, joking, or just trying to see if dumb stories scare me. "We'll wake the dead," I say.

"Pard, if they're around, they'll wake *you*." Zack chuckles at his joke and points with his cigarette. "See that rock? The tall, flat one up ahead?"

Hard to miss. It's enormous. "Yeah."

"That's where they landed."

"Where who landed?"

"Aliens."

"Are you for real?" is what I want to say, but I just say, "No kidding?"

"Hey, this made the *Weekly World News*. I know the guys who saw it."

"Really."

"The aliens gave 'em identical scars on their ankles. I've seen 'em."

"The aliens?"

"The scars. Absolutely identical, one to the other. Like they were branded. It's proof."

"Proof of what?"

"Aliens. No humans could match scars that way." He takes a drag on his cigarette to seal the argument.

"Wait a minute. If you had a branding iron, you could match scars. They'd all be alike, right?"

Zack shakes his head. "Not like these. Nope. You had to see it, pard."

I play along. "So what did the aliens look like?"

"That's the amazing thing. Concealed themselves. Injected Aston and Parr — the guys who saw 'em — with some kind of memory-reduction drug."

"I'll *bet* they were on some kind of drug!" I snort.

"Laugh if you like, pard. All they could remember is they were abducted. And from the waist down their abductors were green and had webbed feet."

I laugh. "You sure they weren't abducted by frogs?"

"Go ahead, act tough. They come down for you, you'll be sayin' your prayers."

I snicker. "I don't think so."

"Tough guy, huh."

"Nope. Atheist."

"You don't believe in God?"

I shake my head firmly.

"You don't believe all this" — he gestures around the lake, and it is kind of beautiful, in a stark way — "was made by a higher power?"

"Yeah. I do."

"Well, there you go, pard."

"The Army Corps of Engineers," I say. "That's the higher power. If they didn't build the dam, we wouldn't be out here. There wouldn't be a lake. This would be a little dried-up creek."

"That's not what I'm talking about, and you know it, pard. Don't believe in God, and don't believe in aliens? I believe the Devil's after your soul. All the same to you, I think I'll take the wheel." He flips his cigarette butt overboard, turns toward the back of the boat, and shouts at my father. "Hey, Dave!"

"Yeah?" Dad hollers over the roar of the engine.

"You ought to teach your son something about the Lord."

"I did."

"Yeah? What's that?"

"That He doesn't exist."

Gilda picks up the conversation. "I don't believe you are saying that! My own uncle!"

"Let's just change the subject, okay?" Dad says calmly.

"You're the one who started with your atheist

130

crap," says Penny. "I don't want the kids hearing that bull."

"Look, I didn't start anything. I'm not telling you what to believe. And I don't want anybody telling me what I should and shouldn't teach my kid, if it's all the same to you."

Zack shakes his head as if Dad and I are the most disgusting pieces of slime he has ever met. But Penny won't let up. She waves her beer can in one hand and her cigarette in the other. "David, you think you're so much better than we are."

"Oh, come on," Dad protests.

"Classical music. Fancy clothes. Atheist. Nothing normal people do is ever good enough for you. Well, let me tell you, that attitude's not going to count for anything around here. Nothing. And it's not going to help Ivan either."

I look down at my cheap swimsuit and beat-up sneakers and wonder what fancy clothes she is talking about. Dad throws his hands in the air. "I give up. You want us to swim back or what?"

Penny tosses her cigarette over the side. "Okay. I've said it. Let's enjoy the day." And of course, now that she's gotten that off her chest, everything is totally poisoned. Her looks could kill Dad and me and maybe a few tarantulas for good measure.

Out there on the water, the boat makes its own breeze, which helps some. But the minute we set foot on land, I realize how hot it really is, probably 110 in the sun, and forget about the shade, because there is no shade. To hear Zack talk on the way up, we're supposed to be getting away from everybody, but the picnic spot's got dozens of people with the same idea as us, all of them in loud powerboats that are now roaring around in the general neighborhood.

As I slather myself with extra sunscreen, Zack asks who wants to ski. The girls are up for it, but I pass. I'm actually not bad at it, and it probably would feel great in this heat, but Zack has had about four beers by now, and I half expect he might drown me and leave me for dead as an infidel. Besides, I wouldn't mind some time alone on dry land. "I'm kind of a spaz at it," I lie.

"Not right now," Gilda sneers. "Right?"

"His favorite song!" Wendy laughs.

"Come on," urges Zack from the boat as he downs another brew. "Give it a shot, pard!"

"No, thanks!" I shout.

"Not right now!" Wendy sings in a taunting voice.

"You got it." I spread out a beach towel, put my Mariners cap over my eyes, and lie back. Ten seconds later my cap and body are drenched. With beer.

"Right now!" Gilda shouts as she and Wendy shriek and run away. I ignore them. I just walk into the lake to rinse the beer off. The water is warm, nice, except for the beer cans and cigarette butts and little oil slicks from the powerboats. I paddle around until I bump into a soda can.

I look up and see Gilda skiing past. She looks better from a distance — graceful even. She waves and shouts at me, but over the roar of the engine I can't hear what she's saying, which is probably just as well.

I go back to the beach and lie in the sun. I think about this crazy high school where I may not even get an education and everybody but Cait and Greb could be totally lame. I think about the Silver Bullet and Western Scoop and Carmody, Nevada, in general. I think about Seattle and wonder what my friends back there are doing right now. I think about crying, but then I think about how much trouble Gilda and Wendy will give me if I do. I begin reading a book about Antarctic exploration. It kind of cools me off.

Dad announces that lunch is ready. As I'm sitting at the picnic table with a mouthful of potato salad, Zack comes in from the boat and plunks a gun down on the picnic table. It's this squat little ugly black thing. Fortunately, it's pointed kind of off in the distance.

"What is *that*?" Dad does not exactly hide his disgust.

"What it looks like," Zack replies.

"Not loaded, I hope?" Dad inquires nervously.

"Safety's on," Zack snorts. "What's good's an empty gun?"

"Yeah, right, Dave," says Gilda between sips of beer. "It's not for decoration."

"What's it for, then?" Dad asks.

Penny sneers. "Give me a break."

"See, pard," Zack drawls, "in a place like this, you never know who might want to make some trouble. Few too many beers. Bad day at the slots. Love problems. You never know. This evens things up."

"What, you'd shoot 'em?" I ask.

Zack must be on his sixth or seventh beer himself. He smiles and shakes his head diagonally. "I want the other fella to consider the possibility."

Somebody changes the subject. We are almost polite to each other all the way through dessert. Afterward, Dad and I clean up while the others go skiing. "Sorry I made you do this," Dad says. "Weird day, huh?"

"Did you hear about the aliens?"

"Some. The engine's real noisy back there."

"I think these people must be aliens," I say. "Beer. Smoking. Guns. Gambling. God. *They're* from Mars."

"News for you, Ivan: They think the exact same thing about us."

"Huh?"

"Believe me. Right now out there on the boat, they're saying, 'These people are totally uptight. They don't smoke, they hardly drink, they never gamble, they don't understand about guns, and they don't even believe in religion.' "

"What a laugh. Basically, they're ignorant."

Dad lets out a big sigh. "In some ways. Sure, there are plenty of things we know that they don't. Somehow I don't think they've heard much Mozart."

"I'd bet on that."

"But don't get too high and mighty about it. There are also plenty of things they know that we don't."

"Yeah? Like what?"

"From what Penny was telling me, Zack seems

to know quite a bit about fixing cars and houses. He certainly knows more than we do about boats. Has to know more than we do about guns."

"And smoking. Drinking. Gambling."

"Look, you don't have to like everybody. It's pretty obvious they don't like us much. But this is a free country. And freedom means something. In this country, people get to do pretty much what they want. We tried outlawing gambling. It didn't work. Most of the states have gambling now."

"Since when?"

"State lotteries? Gambling, right? And if you remember your American history, we tried to outlaw alcohol. That didn't work, either." He takes a sip of beer.

"So what are you saying?"

"I'm saying that there are places in the world where people get thrown into jail for being like us. There are places where people get arrested for being like Zack or Penny. Or whoever. Here the idea is live and let live. We let people screw up if they want to."

"Do we ever!"

"Look at all the tourists who come to Carmody. You can't imagine why. I can't imagine why. But nobody's holding a gun to their heads."

"Except maybe Zack."

Dad chuckles. "Very funny. Seriously: You and I think it's stupid."

"You got *that* right."

"Well, they don't. They think gambling is fun. They like this place. It's what they want. Or think they want."

"So are you saying I should want it?"

"Hey, you know how I feel about conformity."

"So can I ask you one question?"

"Shoot!" Dad says. "Oops — make that 'go ahead.'"

"If nobody here wants what we want, why are we here?"

"Remember what I said about this country allowing people to screw up?"

"Yeah."

Dad frowns. "Maybe I screwed up in a few ways? Maybe I'm slightly irresponsible in my own way? Okay?"

I don't like it when he runs himself down. He doesn't do it very often, but I don't like it. "Come on," I say. "You're not irresponsible."

"There are some things in life I might have done differently."

"Like moving here?"

Dad shrugs. "Look, for now we're stuck here. Make the best of it, okay?"

Stuck is right. Stuck is the word. And stuck goes double for what happens on the way home. Gilda and Wendy are skiing, and Zack keeps his eye more on them than on where we're going. The boat makes this scraping sound, and then a loud thunk, and then we skid to a stop. When we look back, Gilda and Wendy are standing in water up to their ankles.

"Sandbar," Zack says quietly. We're stuck, all right. Marooned. Zack jumps out and looks underneath. The propeller is bent, and possibly some other parts, too, he tells us, along with a whole bunch of swear words.

It's all so absurd that we start to crack up. I mean, the water here's so shallow that Gilda and Wendy just walk back to the boat. Zack is down below, banging on the propeller and swearing. We're all cracking up, even Penny and Gilda and Wendy, but we have to hide it from Zack, because by now he is totally wasted from the beer. He is also really steamed.

"Maybe the Devil got hold of him," Dad whispers to me as we all get out and push the boat back in the water. But the engine won't turn over. It kind of putt-putts and dies.

Zack goes crazier with each new try. He swears. He stomps. He heaves his beer can overboard. And then he takes out his gun and aims at the engine. As we scramble out of the way, he opens fire.

His aim isn't so hot. The engine escapes, but there are a couple of clean bullet holes in the floor of the boat. When Zack sees what he's done, he tosses the gun in the lake. Never in my life have I been happier to see something disappear underwater.

"You're right," I whisper in Dad's ear. "He sure knows a lot about fixing boats."

Eventually we find somebody who's willing to tow us back to the marina. Eventually we manage to convince Zack that he's in no condition to drive his truck back to town. Eventually we get out of the horrendous Labor Day traffic on Entertainment Way. Eventually Gilda and Wendy make some kind of stupid snide remark as I head for the apartment. Eventually I get into the shower to wash up before my shift at the Bullet.

That's when the doorbell decides to ring. I put a towel around my waist and go to answer it. Guess who?

"You pimped me yesterday, man," Greb says. "Festering of you."

"Yeah," I agree. "I felt kind of bad about it. I just wanted to get to know Caitlin a little better. Like alone?"

"Did you?"

I give him my smuggest for-me-to-know-and-you-to-find-out smile.

"You're pimping me again," he half-sings.

"A little," I admit.

"So what about tonight?"

"Date."

"With Cait?"

I nod.

"Where you going?"

"Saturn. Jupiter. Mars."

"Great! You want company?"

"Now who's pimping who?"

"Hey, don't take it so seriously, dude. Joke, man. Listen, just one question."

"Go."

"Did she say anything about my mom?"

I kind of stammer awhile. Then I realize that sooner or later he'll find out that I found out. "Yeah," I admit.

"She's kind of screwed up."

"Cait?"

"Mom."

"Yeah. I heard."

"She's not a nude dancer, man."

"So why did you tell me she was?"

"Hey, dude, no harm meant."

"Okay. Fine."

"I guess I should tell you. Dad's not a brain surgeon. He's a tree surgeon."

"Oh. Wouldn't get much business around here."

"That's for sure."

"So, Greb, why'd you go to all that trouble to make up a story?"

"Hey, come on, man! I didn't want you to think I wasn't interesting."

FOURTEEN

Big Saturday night in Carmody, Nevada. According to Sam, Labor Day is the biggest weekend of the year. Things are so busy at the Silver Bullet that people are actually waiting in line at Western Scoop.

Cait and I are supposed to eat at the Spur Buffet after work. She has made me swear to keep her from going crazy and filling her plate more than half a dozen times. But when we get there, the line is backed up down the hall. We decide there's still plenty of pizza in my freezer.

The parking lot at the Bullet is as full as Caitlin's ever seen it, so her car is all the way up on the roof. It's so crowded that on our way out we get stuck on a ramp. At least it has a pretty good view of The 5 Stars — excuse me, JPCRHS.

"Hard to believe that thing's going to be ready in time," I say. Worklights are still blazing all over the site. Cranes are hoisting debris into dump trucks. Trucks are backing up with their beep-beep-I'm-in-reverse warning. There's still an ugly chain-link fence around the entire place. About the only evidence that the school might get done on time is the sign under The 5 Star Gal. It says **You've never seen a grand opening like this!**

"We'll never see the grand opening, period," Caitlin snorts. "Look at all those trucks! How are they going to be ready for the preview tomorrow?"

"Come on. You know who's going to be featured?"

"Who?"

"Barney Rubble!"

"Seriously, they shouldn't get away with it. If we hand in homework late, we catch hell. Why should we let the school be any different?"

"Maybe they'll give the construction workers D minuses."

"Yeah. Right," Caitlin snorts. "It'll go on their permanent records."

"Maybe they'll make it. The paper says they'll open on time."

"The *Carmody Crier*? Hey, around here, we call it the *Carmody Liar*."

"The preview's still on for tomorrow, so they've got to have the auditorium done. My dad's playing in the orchestra. They're supposed to rehearse there tonight."

"Yeah, I heard. One of the dancers was complaining about it down in the dressing room. She's in the preview, too. She told me, 'I don't know what kind of high school this is going to be, but it's sure not like any one I ever heard of.' Said she hopes her son will learn something besides gambling odds."

"Hey, do you know her name? Maybe I can swap him his Gambling — excuse me, Gaming — for my Comedy."

"Forget it. They don't let you do that. I tried."

"So did you decide what sport you're going to specialize in?"

"Don't remind me. I'm gonna try for administration. You know, like running a team instead of playing on it?"

"That doesn't sound like a bad career."

"If you like sports, it's not, I guess. But I *hate* sports."

It takes us about ten minutes just to lurch out of the parking lot onto Entertainment Way. The street is almost a parking lot itself.

The college guys in the next car over don't mind. The one on the passenger side shouts, "Hey, great car, baby!" and makes kissy faces at Caitlin.

"You know those guys?" I ask.

Caitlin shakes her head. "Suckers. As long as they gamble, they get free drinks. By the time they get out the door, they're barely sane."

"You got that right. Those bozos look like they just crawled out from under a rock."

"I would give them the finger," she tells me, "but I think I'll just concentrate on my driving.

In their condition, no telling what they might do."

"What do you mean, what they might do?"

"I don't know if anybody told you, but a lot of people around here carry guns."

"Yeah, I've heard it, all right," I say. "I've seen it. Does *everybody* around here carry a gun?"

"Hey, baby! Talk to me!" the guy in the next car shouts.

Caitlin ignores him. "I'm telling you, just watch out. All this wild West stuff may be phony, but there are still plenty of people who believe it."

"You look so hot!" the guy shouts.

Caitlin rolls up her window. The guy leans out and taps on it, makes an even more exaggerated kissy face.

"Screw it. *Let* him shoot us." Caitlin gives him the finger. The guys in the car hoot and holler.

Cait sighs. "Saturday night. Drunk night. Not that people are sober other nights. But listen to the radio Sunday morning, and all you hear is people crashed into other people and telephone poles and stuff the night before. They don't even report about all the fender-benders from down here by the casinos."

The light changes. Our hulk moves forward with its usual jerks. The jerks in the next car stay right alongside us. "It's a shame I'm basically a nonviolent person," Caitlin says. "Part of me wants to inflict pain on these morons."

"These guys won't quit," I say, as one of them raps on the window again. "What are we going to do?"

"Watch me!"

Caitlin keeps her cool and looks for an opening. With a mighty lurch, she makes a hard right into the Rancho Rio's valet parking lot. It's a brilliant fake; the other car slams on the brakes and nearly gets rear-ended. With all the traffic on Entertainment Way, there's no way those idiots are going to be able to turn around and find us now.

But we're stuck again, this time behind a crowd of prunies crawling out of their giant Cadillac. A kid in a Mexican outfit taps on Cait's window. She rolls it down.

"Sorry, miss," he says politely. "You'll have to use the self-park. We can't accept cars from anyone under gaming age."

Caitlin flashes her phoniest hotel-employee smile. " 'Scuse us. Guess we goofed."

"No problem," says the valet.

We wait patiently. The instant the last prunie crawls out of the Caddy, the valet jumps in and drives it away with a fast-break tire screech. We're free again.

Caitlin sighs. "Just another romantic night in paradise." We follow the signs back to Entertainment Way. Now we're stuck behind a big motorhome with a Michigan license plate.

I read one of their bumper stickers. "*GOLDEN AGERS DO IT WITH WRINKLES.*"

"Those old folks!" Caitlin waggles her finger at the motorhome. "Only one thing on their minds. Look: *MY KIDS SAY WE SHOULD GIVE UP SEX — IT MIGHT CUT DOWN ON THEIR INHERITANCE.*"

"KISS ME, I'M RETIRED."

Cait smiles at me. "You *wish* you were retired." I try not to blush.

We get past the casinos, break out of the jam, and zoom up to my building. I take Caitlin the back way, to avoid running into Gilda or Wendy, but as we pass the dumpsters, I realize this is totally unnecessary. Gilda and Wendy would be absolutely mortified to show up at the pool on a Saturday night. If they didn't have dates, they wouldn't dream of letting anybody know.

"You haven't exactly made much progress on cleanup," Caitlin observes as we come through the door.

"Hey, we moved one of the boxes just this morning," I say as I head for the freezer.

Cooking is easy, I tell myself. Follow directions. I preheat the oven. I put the pizza inside. I set the alarm on my watch to remind me not to screw up again.

Caitlin and I go into my bedroom to work on the telescope. We finish at pizza hour minus one minute.

"My dad is a big believer in these things," I say as I take the pizza out of the oven.

"My mom can't touch 'em," Caitlin says. "Two slices and she blimps up. Anyway, that's what she says. She thinks she's a blimp if she gains two grams."

"A metric blimp, huh?"

There's a knock on the front door. I hand Caitlin the pizza cutter and head for the door. Somehow I expect the worst.

But it's not the worst, I guess. It's Greb. "Man,

you got any ketchup?" When he spots Cait, he acts surprised. Who knows? Maybe he forgot what I told him. Or maybe he didn't. "Hey, Cait, what's goin' on?"

"Pizza!" she says with her mouth full. She waves a slice in the air. "Want some?"

"Warty!" Greb barges past me and heads for the kitchen.

So much for an interesting evening alone with Cait and pizza and the universe. There are times when you wish your friends wouldn't be so darned polite.

We worry about what Comedy High is going to be like, and when and if it will actually open. The pizza runs out just after we decide we're doomed to a life of permanent failure.

"Ready for the mesa?" Cait asks.

"No way you want to take that scope up there," Greb protests. "Too many weirds."

Cait snorts. "Look who's talking!"

"Seriously, man," Greb says. "It's mellow on weeknights. Weekends kids hang out and drink."

"They can't do that in town?" I ask.

"They like to do it in their own space, you know?" Cait says. "Away from everybody? I hate to admit it, but Greb's right. It can get gross."

"I'm telling you, man," Greb says. "Nothing but trouble up there on the weekends. A friend of mine got stomped. Pustulant!"

"Well, now what?" I grumble.

"The lot?" Greb suggests.

The lot is this vacant patch of sand right beside our building. It's graded for construction, but the developer couldn't raise the money, so now it's just this big flat patch of sand.

I shrug. "Light pollution from the apartments. And the casinos. And Finger. We won't be able to see as much."

"We can see *something*, right?" Greb says.

I stick my head out the door and look up. It's a clear night. When you get down to it, the light pollution in Carmody is no worse than a lot of places. The moon is bright, but that'd be a problem anywhere. "Sure."

"Let's do it," Caitlin says. "We can go to the mesa some weeknight. Besides, who wants to mess with Entertainment Way again?"

We take the telescope out to the balcony. It's easier to line it up if you aim it at something big and bright and fairly close. From here you can't see the casinos, but there's a huge American flag all lit up at a gas station across the river in Finger City. It looks tiny from here, but through the telescope you can just about count the threads in the fabric.

I center the flag in the main scope while Cait checks out the finder. She says the flag is a little to the left, so we trade places. A couple more adjustments and a couple more trades, and we're ready to go. I fold the tripod, hug the scope close to my chest, and carry it down the stairs.

We lug the telescope over to the lot. I set it down, line it up, and use the finder to hunt up my favorite celestial body. It's a little low on the horizon, but still above the worst of the light. I know what I'm doing. It doesn't take me long to find what I'm looking for.

"Okay," I say. "Keep your eye a little bit away from the eyepiece, and whatever you do, don't bump the scope."

Caitlin goes first. It takes her a couple of seconds to adjust her vision. "Saturn?" she half whispers.

"Yeah." I grin, but she can't see it. Saturn always knocks people out. "Good guess."

"The rings," she says quietly. "Wow." As she's about to take her eye away, she leans in again for another look.

"Wow." She steps back, dazzled. The first time I saw it, I was pretty impressed, too. Still am.

Greb steps toward us. "Can I see this thing?"

"Just don't bump it."

"Not me, man." Greb makes a big show of putting his hands behind his back. He leans forward and takes a look. "Warty!" Caitlin whispers to me.

"Pustulous!" I whisper back with a giggle in my voice.

"Very far out!" Caitlin whispers.

But Greb surprises us. "Saturn," he says quietly, shaking his head. "Saturn. Planetary! Hey, impressive, man."

When Greb is done, Caitlin takes another look. "It disappeared!"

"They do that," I say as I readjust the scope. "Remember, they move in the sky."

"False! Wrong! Correction!" Greb shouts. "Actually *we* move, right, Mr. Astronomer? Earth's rotation?"

"When did they teach that on MTV?" I joke,

finding the planet again and centering it in the field.

"Not MTV, man," says Greb. "Third grade."

"Let's hope we learn that much at Comedy High," Caitlin says with a frown. She has another go at Saturn.

"We are going to learn the wonders of entertainment," says Greb. "Let us be positive. Entertain us, Ive."

"Let's see," I say.

Caitlin backs away from the scope. I scan the sky and aim the finder at another bright object. This one's easy.

Caitlin takes a look. "I give up. A big dot and four little ones."

"Planet," I say. "And four moons."

"Jupiter," says Greb matter-of-factly.

"How'd you know that?" Caitlin scowls. "Without even looking?"

"Elementary, my dear gull," says Greb in his perverted version of a British accent. "Jupiter has lots of moons, and most of the very biggest. No problem."

Cait steps back and lets Greb take a look. "Hey," he says. "5 stars."

Caitlin shudders. "Leave it to you, Greb, to come up with exactly the wrong remark."

"Hey, Caitlin," Greb says. "Soon you'll be a 5 Stars Gal."

"A couple more remarks like that," Cait says, "and I am going to send you to the moon."

We look at the moon. We check out a couple of interesting star clusters. We kick the universe around for awhile. Eventually we go back to my place and fire up another pizza.

It's about one in the morning when Dad comes through the door and sniffs the air. "Is there any left?"

Caitlin and Greb and I are just finishing up our third pizza of the evening. She offers Dad the piece she's just cut for herself.

Dad sets his viola case gently on the floor. "You sure?"

"I've only had about seven," Caitlin replies.

Dad thanks her, takes the pizza and a napkin, and heads to the fridge for a beer.

"How was the rehearsal?" I ask.

Dad finishes chewing and takes a gulp of beer before he answers. "Interesting."

"Interesting is one of those words English teachers always tell you not to use," says Cait.

Dad takes another swallow of beer. "Right. Can mean just about anything."

"So what does it mean this time?" Greb asks.

Dad sits down and sighs. "I'm not going to prejudge this for you. Decide for yourselves."

"You're not gonna give us a hint, man?" Greb says disappointedly.

"You guys are up late," Dad remarks, changing the subject.

"Our next-to-next-to-last night of summer," I point out.

"Well, you're not the only ones up," Dad says. "Traffic's still a mess downtown."

I'm kind of amazed. "At one A.M.?"

"Hey, this town just gets rolling at one A.M.," says Greb. "You can go into any casino on a weekend like this, and guaranteed, it's elbow to elbow. People got to get their gambling."

"And I've got to get my sleep," Dad says. "You want to move this party or shut it down?"

We kind of look at each other. "I'm beat," says Greb, draining his can of pop. He stands up and stretches. "Need my beauty rest."

"Me, too," Cait agrees.

"Hey, can we bum rides off you tomorrow? To the show?" Greb asks her.

"It starts at nine, right?" she asks.

"Let's get there early," says Greb. "Get front row seats. It's not every day you get to attend a preview for the wartiest high school on the planet."

"Eight-fifteen?" Caitlin asks. "In front of your building?"

"Sounds good," I say.

"Deal." Caitlin stands up to leave. "Hey, Ive, thanks for the pizza. Mr. Zellner, you too."

"No problem," says Dad. "It's kind of late. Somebody should walk you out to your car."

"Got it covered," Greb says, turning to Caitlin. "I mean, if you don't think it's too pustuliferous."

Cait looks as though she thinks it's slightly pustuliferous, all right, but she says okay. As she and Greb head out the door, I wish I'd thought of offering, but now it's too late. I feel slightly jealous of Greb. But somehow I don't think there'll be any goodnight fooling around.

"Anything new I should know about?" Dad asks once the door closes. The way our schedules overlap, these late-night sessions are sometimes the only chance we have to talk.

I shrug.

"How's the job?"

I shrug again. "Not exactly what I want to be when I grow up."

"How come their parents aren't coming tomorrow night?"

"Greb's mom is supposed to be a little weird. Cait's mom has something else on."

"You got everything you need for school?"

"Mostly. Greb and I are going to the mall at Finger tomorrow."

Dad reaches into his pocket and hands me fifty dollars. "Try not to spend it all, okay?"

Dad is not usually quite this generous just out of the blue. "Geez, did you win a jackpot or something?" I ask.

Dad blushes a little. "You'll never believe this, but I had some spare change in my pocket and a couple of minutes on my hands. Stuck it in a slot machine. Pulled the handle. Bingo."

"How much did you win in all?"

"About a hundred."

"Not bad."

Dad frowns. "It is bad. Lousy willpower. I've got to stay away from those things."

"Not if you win."

"In the long run, you can't win. The whole idea is to keep you gambling. In the long run, the odds wear you down."

"I know," I remind him. "You explained that to me, remember?"

"Well, so-o-o-o sorry!" He laughs. "Anyway, that's what I get for finishing the book I had with me. Next time, I bring two."

"You won't tell me about the show?"

"Same as always. A bunch of almost-naked women sing a bunch of lame songs and pretend to act sexy."

"You know which show I'm talking about."

"What makes you think I'm not talking about the school show?"

"Student's intuition."

Dad looks thoughtful. "I'll tell you just one thing: It won't be what you expect. No matter what you expect."

"I expect the worst."

"Well . . ." Dad trails off.

"Can you explain one thing?" I ask.

"Sure."

"Why don't we move across the river to Finger? I bet they've got a normal high school over there. With science courses instead of Introduction to Gags?"

Dad sighs. "We get a discount on this apartment. Carmody Classic Enterprises gives its employees a deal."

"They don't own anything on the Arizona side?"

"Not unless you work for Pork Power. And the school over there is no prize. From what I hear, they haven't sent anybody to a decent college in years. Remember, there's not a lot of money in Finger. No gambling. No entertainment. No hotels. Carmody sucks up the bucks."

"So it's Carmody for me, huh? And Comedy?"

"Hey, look on the bright side. It could be a lot of laughs."

FIFTEEN

"We are traveling on a journey through space and time," says Dirk Greb the way that guy does on those weird old *Twilight Zone* shows.

"If you pimp me again the way you did last night," I remind him for about the fifteenth time, "I am going to send you on a journey through space and time."

"All right, man, all right. I forgot she was there, remember? Don't rub it in or anything!"

Actually, we are traveling on a journey from Carmody to Finger City. At long last, we are finally aboard the not-very-good ship Li'l Jeeter.

The Li'l Jeeter is this old barge that's decorated to look sort of like an old Mississippi paddle-wheeler, except that on this boat the paddle-wheel doesn't even move. It's just for decoration, like the fake oil lamps on the Carmody Cars.

But if you don't have a real car, you're stuck with the Li'l Jeeter if you want to get to Finger City. The only other way to get there from Carmody is to walk all the way up to the end of town, cross the Winona Carmody Bridge, and walk all the way back down to the part of Finger City that isn't just gas stations. It's about a two-mile walk each way, most of it in the sand right next to a busy highway full of confused prunies trying to keep their RVs on the road. No wonder most people take the five-minute Li'l Jeeter ride instead, even it if does cost a buck-fifty each way.

Of course, there's a catch. When the town is full of suckers, about half a gazillion people are trying to get aboard, and most of them have to find their senior citizen discount cards or their free ride coupons for staying at one of the Carmody Classic Enterprises hotels. So there's a huge line, and we full-fare customers have to stand in the sun and bake with the suckers. "We should've gotten an earlier start," I complain. "Hot as blazes out here."

"Hotter, man," Greb says from under his sombrero. "Hey, you'll get used to it. You'll toughen up. In no time at all you'll be a desert rat. Rodentous!"

Rodentous is what some of these roasting, sweating tourists smell like. I suddenly realize I have never seen so many fat people in one place in my life. "Is there some kind of fatness convention in town?" I whisper to Greb so that no armed fat person will overhear.

"There's always a fatness convention in town," Greb says into my ear. "This is fat people's paradise, man. You can do almost everything sitting down. And then you can hit the buffets and go crazy. I'm telling you: Fat people think they died and went to heaven."

No kidding. As the enormous couple ahead of us steps onto the boat, the thing begins to rock back and forth. They laugh about it. The ticket-taker in the sailor suit with a little picture of Jeeter P. on it looks worried.

Me too. "Hope this scow stays afloat," I tell Greb.

"Hey, don't worry," says the ticket-taker. "You could swim it if you had to."

"Not exactly encouraging," I tell Greb as he leads the way to the front of the boat.

"Don't worry," he says. "This thing hasn't had an accident in a couple of months now."

Two minutes after we leave the dock, he hits me with the line about the journey through space and time.

"Huh?" I say.

"Time travel."

"What, on this thing?"

"You are about to enter a new dimension. It's called the Ari-Zone."

I stare at him, and then I get it. Nevada is in the Pacific Time Zone. Arizona is on Mountain Time. We're halfway across the river, so we're near the boundary.

"You are about to travel backward in time. And then forward again!" Greb proclaims. He stares at his watch. "Follow me. Right . . . about . . . . . . now!"

"2:24!" he shouts, scurrying from the front of

the boat toward the back with me right behind him. "1:24!" he announces. "And now we just wait here, man, and let the Li'l Jeeter carry us ahead one full hour. Amazing, huh?"

"Wait a second," I say.

"A second of Mountain Time, coming right up."

"Arizona doesn't observe Daylight Saving Time!"

Greb scowls. "Are you gonna get technical on me, man?"

"They don't, right? Which means it's the same time on both sides of the river."

"Can I help it if some politicians in Phoenix decided to buck the trend?" Greb says in exasperation. "The point is, it *should* be Daylight Saving Time here. It *should* be one hour later."

"But it isn't."

"Well, it is in winter, man. The day after Daylight Saving Time ends, that river keeps us one hour apart. So pretend. Everybody else does around here."

"Oh, come on."

"And just for bringing up that technicality, you are gonna . . . WALK THE PLANK!"

Greb grabs me and we horse around, but in a couple of seconds the boat is tying up at the dock on the other side and Greb is saying, "Let's beat the crowd."

We're too late. We have to wait in line for the next shuttle bus to the mall, which is the only place you'd want to go in Finger City unless you were up for the Double Strip Dinner. Not that the Finger City Mall is anything special. About the best thing you can say about it is that it's air-conditioned.

Well, there is one more thing about it: It's a Historical Landmark. Greb shows me the plaque that proves this is the first enclosed shopping mall in the Finger City-Carmody region. "Also the only," Greb points out.

And today it's just overflowing with kids. Little kids and their parents, kids our age, older kids. It's the All-American thing to do on Labor Day Weekend — spend money on back-to-school stuff.

Personally, I don't much care for shopping. There's something weird about the air in malls. My Dad claims it's not just stale: They actually pump something in that makes you tired and breaks down your resistance so you'll buy more.

But you can bet a certain cousin of mine thinks the mall is just great. As Greb and I come out of the sports store — just looking, thanks — we run into Gilda and Wendy with a herd of their friends. They have been doing some heavy shopping, all right — particularly shoes, which they are carrying around in boxes, and makeup, which they are carrying around on their faces.

"You didn't buy anything yet?" Gilda greets us. Or greets me. Greb she totally ignores.

"How could we?" I say. "You guys beat us to all the good stuff."

"Very funny." Gilda means it isn't.

"Hey, Gilda, introduce us," says one of the girls.

"Why bother?" Wendy says. "Look who he hangs out with."

"Who?" Greb looks around. "I don't see anybody."

"Forget Greb," says the girl who wanted to be introduced. She points to me. "Who's *this* guy?"

"This is, like, my cousin?" Gilda tells them, accenting the word *cousin* like *gob of subhuman spit*. "His name is, like, Ivan?"

"With a name like that, no wonder he'd hang out with Greb," says one of the other girls.

"And cows." Gilda starts mooing, and Wendy picks up the chant. Giggling, so do the half-dozen other girls with them. I'm just glad I know Cait is working today.

Greb and I walk away. Gilda and her gang are too lazy to bother following us.

"Man!" I say. "There are some people who are just totally impossible!"

"Forget it, man," Greb says. "You can pick your nose, but you can't pick your relatives."

I am about to tell him how Gilda picked her nose — out of a catalog, probably. But before I can get a word in edgewise, Greb says, "Hey, let's get our shopping done and check out the International Museum of Snack Food Technology."

"I thought that was in Carmody."

"Nope. Finger City. Home of Jeeter's Pork Power, the Pork Rind Snacks with the Finger-Snapping Appeal. And the Museum next door. Man, you can't live around here without checking out this place. It's just across the parking lot down at the far end of the mall."

As Greb and I head in that direction, he sees a lot of stuff he wants, but can't afford. Not me. There's plenty of stuff I can't afford, but not much I want. This is because I have inherited some of Dad's shopping genes.

Talk about willpower! Dad has the uncanny ability to speed through just about any mall and ignore anything but the one thing he's there to buy. He hates to shop. When he used to come with me to buy clothes, it was like, hurry up, take anything, let's get going. Now I shop for myself, and I tend to be fussy. Even when I buy a T-shirt, I want to make sure it's going to last.

So Greb and I don't buy much except a couple of burgers and a couple of pairs of shorts. We also buy a couple of pairs of nose glasses. "Ought to freak the teachers out to see 'em on us," Greb says. "And if not, there's always Halloween."

We step out of the air-conditioning and hit the parking lot. Through waves of heat I can see a low building with the sign of the happy pig on top. **Home of Jeeter's Pork Power,** it says, along with the rest of the slogan.

"Where's the museum?" I ask, dodging a car taking a shortcut.

Greb points. "See that shack over there?"

"That's it? That's the whole museum?"

"It's bigger than it looks. It was Jeeter's original factory. He turned it into a museum when they moved next door."

The museum's sign is in the shape of a giant pork rind. As we get closer, I can see the popcorn, peanuts, and potato chips painted on it. **Admission Fifty Cents,** says a little sign on the ticket window by the door. **Includes Snack Size Bag of Jeeter's Pork Power.**

"Your treat," Greb says. "Personally, I don't touch the stuff."

I hand a bill to the pimply guy behind the ticket window beside the door. He's a dead ringer for our town's founding father, except with zits.

"Is he one of the Carmodys?" I ask Greb after I get our ticket stubs and my Snack Size Bags.

"Has to be, man. Could be Jeeter's brother. I mean, talk about pustulous! That guy must live on snack food!"

A little sign on the door says, **Feel free to consume Pork Power within the museum. However, please do not touch the exhibits.**

I open one of the bags and stuff some of the lethal crunchlets into my mouth. "My minimum lifetime requirement of salt, fat, and football hide."

At least it's cool inside. But inside is just one big room. At either end there are enormous beat-up old signs for Jeeter's Pork Power. The rest of the room is full of display cases full of weird stuff arranged in no apparent order.

The first display explains that snacking is a basic biological need. According to the display, humans have eaten snacks ever since the time of the cavemen. "This museum isn't biased or anything," I say.

" 'Course not," Greb agrees.

There's a display on the history of popcorn, from a dried-out old ear of Indian corn to the modern microwave stuff, with some movie-theater popcorn machines and a bunch of home popcorn poppers in between. There's a display on the history of potato snacks, from a sick-looking old spud to modern chips-in-a-can, with lots of old bags and ads and French-frying machines. There's a display on the history of the corn chip from pre-Columbian times to today, complete with a Mexican tortilla machine that looks like something out of a mad inventor's laboratory. There are photos of Great Innovators in Snack Food History, like the eleven-year-old boy who invented the Popsicle, and George Washington Carver, a black guy who invented a million things you could do with peanuts.

Naturally, the biggest display in the place covers the history of the deep-fried pork rind, and, naturally, Jeeter P. Carmody is quoted as saying that it is "Nature's most perfect snack food," though I notice on the Pork Power bag that Jeeter helps nature along with a bunch of chemical flavorings and preservatives. "You know," I tell Greb as we stare at Old Nellie, the pet pig Jeeter P. Carmody owned as a child, "in a crazy way, this is a lot more interesting than I thought it would be."

"Why do you think I brought you here, man?" Greb says. "This is like the one good thing in this whole area. It's history. It's quiet. It's different. It makes you think."

I suddenly realize what's weird about this place: We're the only ones in it. "Right. But where is everybody?"

"Didn't you hear me, man? This place is history. It's quiet. Different. Makes you think."

"I heard you."

"Well, where everybody is is where it's brand-new. Noisy. Ordinary. Doesn't make you think one bit."

"Like Entertainment Way. Or the mall."

"Or," says Greb, "though I sure hope not, Jeeter P. Carmody Regional High School."

SIXTEEN

"Boogerish! Fartitious!" Greb grumbles as we stand in line for the Carmody Car. "In the time it took us to get here from the mall, we could have flown halfway across the universe from the Interplanetary Spaceport."

He's not kidding. We left the mall at about 5:30. It's now 7:30. I've never seen such long lines for anything. A line for the bus. A line for the Li'l Jeeter. And now, a line for the Carmody Car. Which is nowhere to be seen.

"Man, maybe the high school has the right idea," Greb says. "You can't say the tourist business isn't hot."

"Think we'll make it home in time?" I wonder. "We're supposed to meet Caitlin at 8:15."

"I don't know, man. This has got to be the worst traffic jam I have ever seen on Entertainment Way. The absolute pustulest. Getting home's going to be ugly. Getting back won't be any picnic, either."

We hear some honking. Fred Pahinui pulls up in a beat-up old Fiat convertible. "You guys need a ride?"

"No," says Greb. "We're just standing here because we like to breathe exhaust fumes. For our health."

"Get in, will you?" says Fred. "Before the light changes. Or my mind."

Greb vaults over the door and into the front seat. I open the door and get in the back. "You guys going to the preview tonight?" Fred asks.

"You think it's actually going to come off?" Greb says.

Fred points toward the 5 Stars sign. "Check it out! They took down the fence this afternoon. Most of the trucks are gone. I think they're actually gonna make it."

"The question is, are we gonna make it?" says Greb. "This traffic is homicide."

"Two more blocks and it ought to clear up. Hey, Zellner, how do you like the Bullet?"

"It's a job."

"You hear about the Rancho Rio?"

"No. What?"

"Hiring. A dollar more an hour than the Bullet."

"Not bad," I say.

"You ought to go over there and check it out."

"You and everybody else in town," says Greb.

"They're only hiring like ten positions," says Fred. "I heard this from a personal source."

"You and everybody else in the state," says Greb. "Hey, get in there to the left. Big traffic break."

Fred does it without even blinking, and we're moving again. "There's one catch."

"Why did I know that?" I say.

"You have to work seven-day weeks. No exceptions."

"That sounds terrible," I point out. "When do you do homework?"

Fred snorts. "Not my problem, man. But I've got football practice. That's why I can't apply."

"Oh, like you're not going to get homework!" Greb snorts.

Fred smiles. "Whole reason for the Colleges, bud. If you're in Sporting, the teachers are supposed to go easy on you. It's the coaches you've got to watch out for."

Back home, we jump out of the car and run up to our apartments. I take a shower so quick the water conservation board would be proud of me. I change into shorts and my one really outrageous Hawaiian shirt. Sometime I have to ask Pahinui if people in Hawaii really wear these things.

Greb and I meet out on the street as Caitlin's Hulk lurches to a stop in front of us. He has left his sombrero at home, but he's still in his grubbies.

Cait opens the door and lets us in. She's wearing a lacy white dress that she looks great in, which with her figure isn't exactly hard to do. She's wearing makeup and lipstick, but somehow she's a lot less heavy-handed with it than Gilda. "What do you think?" she asks.

"I think you need to get these door handles fixed," Greb mumbles.

I think maybe I should've worn something a little fancier than my Hawaiian shirt and neon shorts, but I don't say that. "Great dress," I say.

"That's the difference between you two," Caitlin says. "One of you is human."

"Hey, proper door handle maintenance is a basic biological need," says Greb.

"Are we *supposed* to dress up?" I ask Cait.

"Nobody said to. I just kind of felt like it."

"I dressed up," said Greb. "Wore my best socks. One hole each."

It's dusk. The sun has gone down, and this orangey-red glow settles over the desert. It's the one time the place looks best, except maybe at dawn, when there's less smog. Of course, the lights from the RV parks and the hotel signs help ugly things up plenty.

As we head toward town, giant searchlights are playing on the sky. "Check it out," says Greb. "We must be inviting aliens from other planets to come to the grand opening preview of Comedy High."

"Right!" I point ahead through the windshield. "Up there! Flying saucers coming to land at the Carmody Interplanetary Spaceport! Aliens!"

"We're the aliens, dude," says Greb.

"How come they're starting this thing so late anyhow?" Caitlin asks. "I mean, school stuff usually starts more like seven."

"Dad says it's so they won't lose a night of casino shows. They just started the hotel shows early so they'd be over in time for us."

"The shows must go on," says Greb.

"They should put you in Performing," says Cait.

The 5 Stars, or maybe it's JPCRHS, definitely has a different look when we drive up. The chain-link fence is gone. The construction equipment is mostly gone, and the lot is paved, painted with fresh lines. For the first time at night, the sign is lit up from top to bottom, and right below The 5 Star Girl and **Carmody High School** it says **SNEAK PREVIEW TONIGHT 9 PM! ALL WELCOME!**

"Great," says Greb. "We'll get a bunch of tourists looking for a free show."

And as we walk through the lot, it actually looks that way. Either that or some of our students or parents are about ninety years old and have to get around with metal walkers. "Excuse me, son," says this geezer as I get out of the car. "Is this hotel new? It's not in last year's triple-A guide."

"It's not a hotel," I say politely. "It's our new high school."

"High school?" the guy's wife snaps. "It looks like a hotel."

"It used to be a hotel," Caitlin puts in.

"No gambling, then?" the man asks.

Greb shakes his head. "Only on our future careers."

"Huh?" the woman says.

"No gambling," Caitlin replies sweetly. "Sorry."

"You're sure?" the man demands. "No slot machines?"

"Positive," I say.

"Well, shinplasters!" says the geezer. Actually he doesn't say that. You expect older people to say something corny like "shinplasters," but what he actually says is only four letters, one syllable.

"Good luck!" Caitlin sings as the old folks totter back to their car. She'd be great in Hospitality.

We approach the volcano in the entrance courtyard. "Bummer," says Greb. "Still not working."

"At least it's uncovered," Cait notes.

"Uncovered isn't working. It's just sitting there. It's supposed to spout water and live flames and stuff. I mean, what good is it to name your sports teams after a volcano that doesn't go off?"

I nod. "I can see it now: people chanting 'No fire in the Volcanoes.'"

"Bummer," Greb repeats. "It's supposed to be ready for the opening."

We make our way to the front entrance. A guy in a tuxedo looks Caitlin up and down as he holds the door open for us. I begin to think this Hawaiian shirt may definitely have been a bad move.

"Doorman. Classy," Greb mutters as we step inside the hotel.

Except it isn't a hotel anymore. It's our new high school. Except it doesn't look anything like a school. We're standing in a huge room. Huge crystal chandeliers — actually, when you look at them a second time, they've got to be plastic — drip from the ceilings. The walls are soft pink. The carpet's got a little five-star pattern on it, and it's kind of worn in places, but who ever heard of a school with carpets?

Or slot machines? Or roulette wheels? Or wheels of fortune? Or blackjack tables or crap tables or keno displays or a TV screen maybe twenty feet tall? We can see all those behind a set of velvet ropes.

"Are we in the right place?" I whisper to Caitlin.

"I wonder," she whispers back.

"Aw, man," says Greb disgustedly as he takes it all in. "They ruined this! This used to be so cool!"

"Still looks like a casino to me," Caitlin says.

"Pustulence, man! They changed everything! There used to be twice as many slots and tables. They used to have a humongiferous 5 Stars sign in neon right there in the middle. And they took out every single one of the statues of naked women!"

"Oh," says Caitlin. "Bummer."

In front of the velvet ropes is a **NO SMOKING** sign. "First one of those I've seen since I moved here," I say.

"You'd think this was a school or something," Greb mutters.

A sign right beside it says **Carmody High Preview Night — Astral Showplace,** with an arrow pointing off to the right. We follow it down a long curved hall.

At the right is a series of offices. "That used to be the reception desk," Greb says.

At the left is a fish tank that runs the entire length of the hall. "That was once the fourth-largest salt-water tank in the free world," Greb informs us. "Used to have fish and girls in mermaid outfits."

"So what happened to the fish?" Caitlin asks.

"I heard something about that," Greb says. "I think they're trying to get somebody to donate some."

"What happened to the girls?" I ask.

"I heard something about that," Greb says. "I think they're trying to get somebody to donate some."

We pass beneath a sign that says **Astral Showplace** in dirty old letters and **Jeeter P. Carmody Auditorium** in bright new ones. A bunch of men in tuxes and women in fancy dresses are standing around in the entryway.

"Welcome!" says a little bald guy. "Tom Colacello, your principal. Glad you could make it."

We shake hands and introduce ourselves.

"You people looking forward to getting back to school?" Colacello asks.

Caitlin and I hesitate. Greb saves us. "About as much as I'd look forward to rattlesnake pizza."

"Well, maybe we'll change your mind," says our new principal.

"Maybe," says Caitlin. "Are we really going to learn anything useful here?"

"That's up to you, isn't it?" says Colacello, still smiling.

"Good answer!" Greb cries. He's a big fan of *Family Feud*.

"Good luck!" Colacello replies. "Let's hope we next see each other under similarly happy circumstances."

He welcomes a couple of kids who have just come in behind us. We move on toward Mr. Seacrist, who is wearing a tux. He gives us an insincere hello and hands us off to Ms. Rudge. She squinches her pinched little face into something like a smile and hands us each a program. "We think you'll be pleased with your new school," she says as though she's memorized it.

"Zooks! Which pickle barrel did they find her in?" Greb says.

"Somehow I bet she wasn't in the picture with the nose glasses," Caitlin murmurs.

"She's the one who gave me my test," I tell them.

"No wonder you got assigned to Comedy," Caitlin says, as we step through the door to the auditorium.

The auditorium is empty. And enormous. The curtain across the stage is dark blue with stars painted all over it. "Not bad, huh?" Greb says. "Famous people have played here."

"Like who?" I ask. "Elvis?"

"You *wish*, man. Hey, when Elvis was alive, Carmody was a bunch of sagebrush."

"Elvis *is* alive," I retort. "Seen at a UFO convention. You ought to read those newspapers at your market!"

"I'm talking *stars*, man," says Greb. "Bill Moonbeam. Conley Van Rense. Monica Landon."

I snort. "Never heard of any of them."

"You think somebody's not famous just because *you* haven't heard of him?"

I wince. "I thought the whole point of being

172

famous was that people are supposed to have heard of you."

"Yeah. People in general. Not Ivan the Zellner."

"Hey, look!" Caitlin points to the ceiling. It's a deep midnight blue, and stars twinkle all over it, and the man in the moon smiles down. There's only one chandelier, a huge one shaped like the sun. The planets go around it.

"Wartitious!"

We find seats in the front row. "Not your usual high school auditorium," Cait points out.

I get up and lean over the orchestra pit. Greb follows me. Nobody's down there. "Where's your old man?"

I shrug. "Early yet."

We sit down again. Caitlin shows me her program. Basically it's a list of all the politicians in town and all the high school administrators and casino officials. There's also a little history of the 5 Stars, from Jeeter P. Carmody turning over the first shovel of earth to pictures of not-so-famous famous people such as Bill Moonbeam, Conley Van Rense, and Monica Landon. The rest of the program is ads for the casinos, the markets, and Jeeter's Pork Power. "Warty program," Greb says. "Doesn't even tell you what you're going to see."

"Not unless Bill Moonbeam shows up," I say.

We look around. People are arriving behind us. Some are dressed up, but a lot aren't, so I don't feel totally stupid. Just mostly stupid.

But nobody comes down front to our row or

173

even the row behind us. Everybody else is at least five or six rows back, except for some adults in tuxes — like Ohio Bob, the guy who hired me at the Silver Bullet.

"How come nobody else is sitting up here?" Cait asks.

"Wimps. Wusses," says Greb.

"I wonder if these seats are reserved or something," I suggest. "You know, for the teachers and honored guests and stuff."

"I didn't see any signs," says Caitlin.

"We're ice, man," Greb insists. "Stone frigid. Polar."

Which is true. Until Rudge arrives. Talk about ice! "What are you three doing here?"

"Waiting for a Carmody Car," Greb says politely.

Rudge points behind us. "Why do you think there are no students in front of row F?"

"No initiative," Greb says.

"Can you read?" Rudge whines.

Greb shakes his head. "I'm a failure of the educational system."

"You're sitting in the reserved section," Rudge informs us.

"Where does it say that?" Caitlin asks.

"There's a sign?" Rudge wheezes. "It says **RESERVED.**"

I give her a look of disbelief. "I didn't see any sign."

"Me neither," Greb and Caitlin agree.

"Well, you go back there and look. The first five rows are reserved for honored guests."

And they are, of course. When we go back up the aisle, we have to move a rope with a **RE-SERVED** sign on it that's stretched across the back of row five. "Nice," Caitlin says. "They put this up after we got here."

"Look at it this way," I say. "For an all-too-brief moment, we were actually honored guests."

"Yeah, what the hey," says Greb. "Still plenty of seats." We find new ones under the planet Mars.

People are coming in thicker and faster now. It's a strange mix. Some kids arrive in bunches. Some come as couples, hand in hand or with their arms around each other's waists. Then there are whole families who come in together. The dignitaries in suits and tuxes and formal gowns head for the reserved seats, but so do a few people who aren't dressed much better than I am.

There even seem to be a few tourists, people who wander in thinking this is a hotel. They tend to go down an aisle and look around and suddenly realize something's out of whack, maybe all the kids and the fact that nobody charged them to get in. They look puzzled, a little like this classmate of mine in Seattle when she accidentally stumbled into the boys' bathroom.

People wave hello at Caitlin and occasionally Greb. The only people who recognize me are Sam Chandresekar, who gives me a little salute when his parents aren't looking, and Fred Pahinui, who seems to be saying hello to everybody. Then Gilda sashays in with Wendy and the rest of their crowd, all dressed up and made up, looking completely phony compared to Cait, and of course, snubbing us totally.

I get this awful feeling in the pit of my stomach. I'm especially worried for Caitlin. I can just hear Gilda's gang mooing in front of the whole crowd.

But then Zack and Penny and more adults follow right behind, so I figure Gilda won't dare make a scene.

I let out this big sigh. "I know, man, I know," Greb whispers in my ear. "I was thinking the exact same thing."

SEVENTEEN

The auditorium goes dark. A spotlight splashes a huge American flag as it drops down in front of the curtain. "Ladies and gentlemen," booms a deep announcerish voice from nowhere and everywhere, "Will you all please rise as we salute America with the playing of our national anthem?"

"What's next? A ball game?" Greb mutters.

As we rise to our feet, the orchestra swoops up from the pit on a giant elevator platform. A second spotlight picks out the conductor, and by the lights on their music stands you can see the musicians, all dressed in black. "Your dad looks cute in the tux," Caitlin whispers.

The conductor gives the downbeat and we hear the "Oh, say, can you see?" music at a fast, upbeat tempo. Some people sing along. Some, like Caitlin and me, just stand there. Some put their hands on their hearts. And some, like Greb, put their baseball caps on their hearts. When it's over, there's a big round of applause, the flag disappears, the orchestra vanishes, and everybody sits down again.

"Ladies and gentlemen," booms the voice again, "Mr. Jeeter P. Carmody!" The audience applauds, and the curtain goes up. Standing in a spotlight at the far left of the stage is the guy whose name and face are famous for miles around. But in his tuxedo he seems different from the way he does on television. He's quiet, soft-spoken, almost shy. You have to strain to hear him.

"Folks, a lot of people wondered what the heck we were doing with this thing. A lot of people wondered whether we'd ever get it accomplished. And there are still a few things left undone. Just one example, let me tell you: We're gonna have so many fish out there in that tank by the end of next week that you'll think you're in Davy Jones's Locker Room."

"That's locker, dimwit!" Greb mutters. "Not locker room!"

I laugh. "You ever smell Davy Jones's locker room?"

"There are other things that need some final touch-ups," says Jeeter, "but that's business. Some people never get things done when they say they will. But some people never have dreams, either. Well, I had a dream, and I believe in my dreams. And now — well, now, we're gonna show you one dream that became reality!"

Jeeter's spotlight goes dark. Brassy music hits our ears, and a spotlight opens up the other end of the stage. Five men and five women dressed in cowboy outfits begin to dance and sing:

> He had a dream.
> He had a dream.
> Jeeter P. Carmody had a dream
> And he called it the Carmody Inn.

A picture of the Carmody Inn flashes onto a huge screen at the back of the stage.

> He had a new dream.
> He had a big dream.
> His second dream was
> For a big new bridge,
> And he named it after his mom.

Greb leans over and whispers in my ear. "Apparently this school is not going to feature a class in rhyming."

As he says this, the dancers turn themselves into a human bridge that mimics the one on the screen. Then more dancers appear, in costumes that look like hotel buildings with feet.

> He had a bigger dream.
> He had an amazing dream.
> His third dream was
> Of a shining city,
> And he called it Carmody, Nevada.

179

"The Silver Bullet costume is definitely the best," Caitlin whispers to me.

"The volcano gets my vote," I whisper back.

> He had the biggest dream yet.
> He had a dream for the future.
> He had a dream for the kids of Carmody, Nevada.
> He had an American Dream
> For American Teens . . .

American Teens? Caitlin, Greb, and I make barfing gestures. And three thumbs down.

> . . . And now it's for real!
> Yes, now, now, it's HERE!

The dancers rush to the front of the stage and fling their arms out at the audience as if to say, "Look around you!" A few people start clapping, and then the lights go on in the auditorium and the announcer says, "Ladies and gentlemen, a big Jeeter P. Carmody Regional High School hand for the most important part of our new educational facility — the student body!"

The dancers start clapping to lead the biggest round of applause yet. People in the audience stamp their feet and hoot and holler with big Western "Ya-hoos!"

Greb puts his hands under his legs. "Hey, I didn't come here to salute myself, man. I can do that at home."

When the applause dies down, so do the lights in the auditorium. "Ladies and gentlemen," booms the announcer again. "The principal of Jeeter P. Carmody Regional High School: Dr. Tom Colacello!"

The spotlight hits the stage again, and there's the little bald guy we met in the hall. He's still in his tux, but now he's holding a microphone. "Well, we made it!" he says. "Do you like what you've seen so far?"

"Yeah!" shouts most of the audience. The firm of McKibbin, Zellner, and Greb isn't willing to commit itself.

Colacello puts his hand to his ear. "Can't hear you!"

"Yeah!" the audience (except for us) shouts louder.

"Still can't hear you!"

"Yeah!" the audience (except for us) roars.

"All right!" cries Colacello. "Now we're going to show you what your new school is all about!"

The spotlight fades. When the lights go up, you can see a ratty, ancient-looking shack. Two raggedy-looking people, a man and a woman, stop at the door beneath a sign that says **Inn**. They look familiar somehow.

"I hope they have room, Joseph," says the woman, who is very pregnant.

"I do, too, Mary," says the tall guy with her.

"Jesus!" Greb mutters.

"Close," Caitlin says.

Joseph knocks on the door. A big, surly guy in tattered clothes opens it. "Come, come, man! What is it?" he screams in Joseph's face.

"Would you have a room for the night?" Joseph asks politely, desperately.

"No! We're out of rooms!" the guy screams. "We're full! Get lost! Scram!" He slams the door in Joseph's face.

The lights dim, and the spotlight comes up on a woman in a formal gown. "If only he'd attended the College of Hospitality Arts and Sciences, things might have been different."

The spotlight fades. When the light goes up on the inn again, it looks as though it's had a fresh coat of paint. Joseph knocks on the front door. The same big guy opens the door, but this time he's wearing a tux and he's had a personality transplant. "May I help you, sir?" he asks.

Joseph nods humbly. "Would you possibly have a room for the night?"

"Certainly, sir," says the innkeeper with a polite bow. "What kind of accommodations would you prefer?"

"Nothing fancy," says Joseph. "We're on a budget."

"I understand. Empress or emperor bed?"

"Is the emperor a lot more expensive?"

The innkeeper displays all his teeth. "Just a few pieces of silver."

"I think the empress will do, dear," says Mary.

"Spitting or non-spitting?"

"Non, I think," says Joseph.

"River view?" asks the host.

"Oh, anything at all will be fine," Mary replies.

"Bite your tongue, ma'am!" says the innkeeper. "Nothing's too good for *our* customers. Why, some varlets couldn't care a fig for your comfort. For all they care, some of them might as well rent you a manger!"

There's a ripple of laughter as the lights go down and the spotlight comes up on the woman in the gown. "The College of Hospitality Arts and Sciences," she says. "Where rudeness is . . . history."

As the audience applauds — this time it includes us — the announcer's voice says, "Meet the distinguished faculty of the College of Hospitality Arts and Sciences."

The lights come up. The announcer introduces the woman in the gown, who turns out to be Hospitality's vice-principal. The actors turn out to be teachers, and they come forward as the announcer introduces them.

"Hey, man, not suppurating," says Greb.

"Not even bad," Caitlin agrees.

The rest of Hospitality comes out for a moment in the spotlight. When they leave the stage, the lights go down and hard-driving music comes up.

When the lights come up again, the stage has turned into a gym. We see a long line of people's backs turned to us, every one decorated with the green-and-orange Volcanoes insignia of an official Carmody High jacket. Suddenly everybody makes an explosive 180-degree turn and starts exercising and singing to a rap beat.

> We're the Volcano Coaches
> And we're gonna rock you!
> We're the Volcano Coaches
> And we're gonna sock you!
> We coach the Volcanoes
> And we hate to be abrupt,

But Volcano Sports are about to erupt!
At the College
Of Sporting
Arts and
Sciences!

"Hey, these are your guys!" I tell Caitlin.

"Don't rub it in," she says, "Look at those bodies! They sure don't hang out at the buffets."

The rap beat keeps going, but the singing stops and the tune changes to "Take Me Out to the Ball Game." Three women and three guys do some pretty decent gymnastic routines. At one end, a huge guy at a hoop hits slam dunk after slam dunk until a couple of women in basketball outfits foul him to the floor. A bunch of football players work a pass play. A man and a woman jump over hurdles. A couple of guys clash with hockey sticks. Half a dozen women display some pretty fair soccer footwork. Finally, everybody lines up to hit these foam baseballs into the crowd. I nearly catch one, but the kid in front of me leaps in the air to snag it.

We're the Volcano Coaches
And we're gonna rock you!
We're the Volcano Coaches
And we're gonna sock you!
We coach the Volcanoes
And we hate to be abrupt,
But Volcano Sports are about to erupt!
At the College
Of Sporting
Arts and
Sciences!

184

"Not repetitious or anything," Greb mumbles as a pudgy guy in a striped referee uniform comes out and blows a whistle. Everybody freezes, and the curtain comes down to wild applause. Then the curtain goes up again, and the announcer introduces the Sporting faculty.

"I bet the referee's the vice-principal," says Caitlin.

It turns out she's right. "Hey, there's your future career," I tell her.

"What? Vice-principal?"

"Referee."

Caitlin puts her hands around my neck and mock-strangles me.

The curtain goes down, and this guy in a dealer's outfit — you know, string tie, suspenders — saunters out in front of it. "Ladies and gentlemen, place your bets!" he says as the curtain rises and the music swells.

Now the stage has turned into a casino. In the background, people are gambling on the usual slot machines and games. At the left is a huge TV screen with sports scores from across the country.

As the dealer walks up to the roulette table, the scores disappear from the TV screen. Instead we can see the roulette table — and a little scoreboard marked **RED** and **BLACK**, with $10 under each one.

The dealer explains how the table is laid out. Half the numbers are red and half are black — except for 0 and 00, which are green. "Your programs have a little dot on them — either red or black. That's the side you're betting on — ten imaginary dollars at a time. Now which one have you got? Shout it out!"

"Red!" screams half the audience — including Caitlin. "Black!" screams the other half — my half. Somewhere in there Greb screams "green!"

The TV picture closes in on the roulette wheel. The dealer spins it and tosses the ball in. We holler "Red!" and "Black!" (and, in Greb's case, "Chartreuse!") at the top of our lungs as the ball drops down toward the spinning part of the wheel and bounces around. "All right!" says Cait as the ball drops into the 12 slot. It's red. She's up to twenty bucks. I'm down to zero.

The dealer lets our side go into negative numbers — ten bucks worth — as red wins the next spin, too. But we get ours back as black takes the next three. The hollering gets even louder — people are on their feet, shaking their fists — as red comes through with four in a row. We end up even, back where we started — but in a silly, mindless way, it's actually been kind of fun.

"Are you excited?" the dealer hollers.

"Yes!" the audience shouts back.

"Well, that's what Gaming is all about!" The dealer takes a bow, and then the Gaming faculty follows.

The curtain comes down again, and the spotlight picks up two masks, one happy and one sad, high above the stage. According to the announcer, what we see next is a scene from Shakespeare's *Romeo and Juliet*. Juliet is up on the balcony, and Romeo is downstairs looking up at her, and they talk about how much they love each other even though their families hate each other's guts. It's a little hard to follow if you haven't seen the rest of the play, but even in the old-fashioned setting and way-ancient clothes, the actors are so emotional and so good-looking they really do make you believe they're in love with each other.

"I can just see Performing Gilda in that!" I snort.

"She'd be great," Caitlin says. "She's so in love with herself, she'd have to play both parts."

Suddenly the whole stage revolves, and we're on a modern city street. "Another version of the same romance," the announcer proclaims. "Leonard Bernstein's *West Side Story!*" This couple sings a song called "There's a Place for Us." I've heard it before, and it's not my kind of music — too dippy and syrupy — but the sadness in it gets to me anyhow. Caitlin, too: As the song ends, I'm pretty sure she's got a tear in her eye. I spare her my snotty remarks.

The stage revolves again, and we're out West for what the announcer says is a ballet from Copland's *Billy the Kid*. The dancers are some of the same ones we saw in the opening song about Jeeter P.

I know this music, too, because Dad has played it, but it's the first time I've seen people dance their way through a shootout. It's actually pretty exciting. And moving. "Got to admit," says Greb as the stage spins again, "cooler than I'd've guessed."

Now the stage is empty except for a tall, bony, black woman with long dark hair that spills over the shoulders of her tuxedo and glitters in the spotlight. As mysterious music begins, she makes a broad gesture with her hands. From out of nowhere, a long wand appears between them.

"Warty!" Greb cries, impressed.

As she waves the wand, it turns into a bouquet of red roses. The crowd applauds, and she bows slightly. "I am . . . Delilah. And it's time for the magical part of our program." She turns backstage and hollers. "Dr. Colacello? Dr. Colacello?"

Our principal steps into the spotlight, and Delilah hands him the roses. "These are for you."

"Thank you," says Colacello.

"Don't mention it," she replies, and just like that, the roses vanish from his hands. The crowd cracks up.

"How'd you do that?" Colacello says.

"I was hoping you'd ask," answers Delilah with a touch of menace. "I'm going to show you." She steps forward and talks to us almost confidentially. "Ladies and gentlemen, I am about to perform an illusion that's extremely popular in every school I visit."

"What's that?" Colacello asks.

Sparks shoot from Delilah's fingertips. "I am about to make the principal . . . disappear."

As the crowd howls, she whips out this big sort of fabric tube and drapes it over Colacello's body. She pulls it up so you can't see him any more, but you can still see the lumps he makes in the fabric. The orchestra sends up a drumroll as Delilah says some magic words and waves a wand at the tube. "Still there?" she asks.

"Sure am!" replies Colacello's voice from the tube.

Delilah shakes her head and tries again. "Still there?"

"Haven't gone anywhere!" says the principal's voice.

The drumroll is even louder this time as Delilah works her magic. "Still there?"

And then, I swear, don't ask me how, Colacello steps out from the wings and says matter-of-factly, "No, now I'm over here."

The crowd claps its hands off as Delilah whips the fabric tube through the air to prove it's empty. "It's like my mama always told me," she says, "If you have good solid principles, nothing can ever make *them* disappear!"

The curtain comes down to the biggest round of applause yet. The lights go up and the Performing faculty takes its bows.

When they're done, the lights dim once more and the announcer introduces "Mr. Joe 'Killer' Logan!" A wiry redheaded guy with a pointy goatee and a slightly demonic look stands in front of the curtain. "Now, ladies and germs, it's time for the serious part of our program."

He stares out at us. For a long time. "Comedy," he finally says.

There are a few laughs from the crowd. Greb elbows me. "Here we go."

"I'm serious. Comedy is serious business." Logan says. "You don't believe me? Come on. Let me show you."

The curtain goes up on a laboratory. People

are busy working with all sorts of equipment. "This is the comedy test lab," says Logan. "This is where we try out our ideas. Take McGlinn, here. He's a comedy writer."

"I don't know," the guy whines. "I'm working on this idea, and I just don't know if it's funny."

"Try it on me," Logan says.

"You sure?" McGlinn asks.

"Of course. That's what I'm here for."

McGlinn takes out this tiny sledgehammer, winds up, and hits Logan on the head with it. For some reason the way he does it, and Logan's deadpan reaction are just hilarious. Logan turns to us and says, "Funny?"

Through our laughter we holler back, "Yes!"

"Funny," Logan says.

"Thanks," replies McGlinn.

Logan heads for the next desk, where an older woman with glasses is fiddling with something we can't see. "Problem, Ms. Wilgus?"

The woman holds up a seltzer bottle. "This just doesn't seem to work anymore."

"Out of laughs?"

She shrugs. "Maybe you can get some out of it."

Logan takes the bottle and aims it at her. "Sure, now?"

"Go ahead. Try. I can't find any laughs in there."

Logan aims again, "Okay. One . . . Two . . . Three!" He pushes the trigger, and water gushes out — all over *him*. It's hysterical.

"See?" says Ms. Wilgus. "You got the laugh. Not me."

"Needs a little more research," says Logan. He wipes his face with his handkerchief and moves on. There's a table with three pies on it and a gangly guy behind them.

"See? Serious business." Logan says. "Mr. Farnsworth here is studying the theory of the pie."

"Gooey ones," Farnsworth says somberly. "Lots of comedy in these."

Suddenly Dr. Colacello walks in from offstage. "Are you guys almost done? We've got to wrap up the show."

"Well, it's not as easy to get a laugh as it used to be," says Logan. "We're doing research."

"Can I help?" Colacello asks innocently.

Logan and Farnsworth stare at us. We all crack up. "Just stand there," Farnsworth tells our principal.

"Where?" Colacello asks.

Logan gets behind him and grabs him by the shoulders. "Right . . . here. That okay, Farnsworth?"

"A little closer," Farnsworth replies.

Logan moves Colacello again. "That good?" he asks.

"Perfect," says Farnsworth, picking up the pie with an evil look in his eye.

"So what do I have to do now?" says Colacello.

"Just stand there while I count to three," says Farnsworth. "One . . . two . . . !"

We all gasp. He doesn't wait for "three" to toss the pie. And then we gasp again: Colacello ducks, and Logan's the one who gets a faceful of goo!

Logan turns to us and wipes a hole where his

mouth is. "I'm telling you — comedy is serious business!"

"This may turn out to be okay after all," I tell Greb as the Comedy faculty comes out for its bows.

"No worse than Willsman, that's for sure," he says.

"You guys are so lucky," says Cait as the curtain goes down and the house goes dark. "If I could change, I would do it in a minute."

The music swells up with the Pork Power theme. "Ladies and Gentlemen," says the announcer, "Mr. Jeeter P. Carmody."

Jeeter turns up at center stage. "What do you think?"

The applause starts at kind of low volume, but it keeps getting louder and louder as Jeeter calls everybody back onstage and people start getting up and giving the whole faculty a standing ovation. Even Greb is on his feet, though he somehow manages to stay cool about it.

I can't exactly explain it, but there is something at least as magical now as when Delilah made the principal disappear. We feel as though we're part of something, and that something is beginning to look pretty good.

Jeeter keeps saying, "Excuse me" and waving his hands to quiet the crowd, but nobody is ready to quit applauding yet. The teachers are exchanging these smiles that don't seem phony, smiles that look as though they really believe we might be worth teaching. Then they start applauding us.

We applaud back in chunky rhythms. The

orchestra rises on the elevator, and though you wouldn't think the applause could possibly get louder, somehow it does. It's not necessarily that we believe everything is going to be great. It's that we want to believe it, and right now it almost seems possible.

Finally Jeeter gets everybody to settle down. "We're done here in this fine auditorium, but we're not *all* done," he says. "We think this school has students and teachers like nobody else in the world. Now, please join us outside in the main entrance courtyard, and we'll share something we're positive no other high school in the world can match."

"The volcano?" Caitlin asks.

Greb shrugs. "Either that or the world's largest bag of Pork Power."

EIGHTEEN

Forget the volcano. Forget the Pork Power. What we have right now that no other high school in the world can match is the feeling that's in the room. It may only last for the evening. It might die the minute the teachers have to start worrying about attendance and tests and hall passes instead of entertainment. But who knows? Maybe they'll find a way to make attendance and hall passes fun, and hey, I've always kind of enjoyed tests anyway.

As we walk out of the auditorium to recorded music from that *Billy the Kid* ballet, we still have this kind of glow on our faces and in our hearts. It's corny, but it's real. We feel good. Everybody's smiling.

"Got to admit. Not too pustulous," says Greb

as we make our way through the crush in the hallway.

"Maybe Sports won't be so bad," Caitlin sighs. "At least they seem to have a sense of humor."

"And the air-conditioning works in here," I point out. "At least we won't fry in class."

As we file out, Gilda and Wendy pass us on the left. I shudder a little, expecting trouble. But all Gilda does is smile and gush. "Told you! Told you! Didn't I tell you it was going to be super-ex?"

I smile back. "Got to admit it."

"This is going to be so cool?" Wendy says.

"Polar," I say.

"Hey, man, let's not get carried away," Greb says, but he says it with a grin.

Everybody's so *up*. It's like the feeling after a ball game where your team has just won a tough one. People are laughing, joking, feeling good about the world.

Even Dad has caught the spirit. "Better than I expected, that's for sure," he says, catching up with us at the edge of the casino area. "What'd you think?"

"Not pustulous," I say before Greb has a chance to.

"How come you didn't want to tell us about it beforehand?" Cait asks him.

"Believe me, it didn't look so hot in rehearsal," Dad says. "It was a mess last night. They whipped a lot of this into line since then. Hard work. There's no substitute."

Greb grins. "Unfortunately for humanity."

Dad laughs. "You got that right."

We're out the door now, gathering in the courtyard. The spotlights make a dome of light high in the sky. Colored lasers play on the volcano.

"Have you guys ever seen this thing work?" Dad asks.

"Did you? At rehearsal?" I ask back.

Dad laughs. "I heard they rehearsed this thing about five in the morning."

"I've never seen it," Caitlin says. "This place was already closed down when we first moved here."

"I've seen it," Greb says.

"And?" Dad asks.

"Hey, man, I wouldn't want to prejudge it for you."

Everybody is out in the courtyard now. A spotlight plays on Jeeter P. as he climbs up to a little platform. "Ladies and gentlemen, Mr. Jeeter P. Carmody!" Greb and Caitlin and I murmur. We crack up as the announcer echoes our words.

"Thank you, thank you," says our founding father. "I hereby dedicate the symbol of our new spirit: the Jeeter P. Carmody Regional High School . . . Volcano!" The crowd roars as Jeeter presses the button. And then the volcano does a little roaring of its own.

The first thing we hear and see is an enormous jet of water shooting up toward the sky, pulsing higher and higher. "When I went to school, volcanoes were supposed to be *hot*," Dad says.

Greb grins. "Wait."

The jet of water lowers and turns into a sort of circular waterfall around the edge of the volcano. Little mini-jets make patterns in the colored light.

"We're waiting," Caitlin says.

Suddenly there's a *whoosh!* and then a roar, and a giant tongue of flame shoots into the sky where the jet of water used to be. It's such a surprise that you can almost hear the crowd sucking in its breath all at once.

Little flames somehow appear in the waterfall. "Fire on water," says Greb quietly, mimicking the announcer. "A reminder of America's greatest oil-spill disasters."

The jet of water shoots up again. Then comes the jet of flame. Then the jet of water. And then more flame, this time with sputtering, dancing sparks.

Except something goes wrong. The wind blows some of the sparks toward the crowd on the opposite side of the volcano from where we are. The people over there jump back, but they're standing under this sort of canopy at the entrance, so they're okay.

They're okay, but the canopy isn't so hot. Or rather, it is. There are construction tarps on top, and as the sparks land on them, they turn into little tongues of flame. "Hey! Cut the volcano!" somebody shouts.

"Right! Shut it off!" Dad yells.

Other people take up the cry, but nobody seems to hear. Up on his little platform, Jeeter picks up the microphone, but apparently it's gone dead. "Man!" mutters Greb. "Man!"

A cry of "Fire!" ripples through the crowd. The volcano keeps putting out new sparks, the wind keeps blowing them toward the tarps on the canopy, and the crowd under it is scattering everywhere except straight toward the volcano where the sparks are coming from.

The tarps are ablaze now, but everybody's gotten away. The volcano has stopped sputtering flames. It's down to just water.

A tall, bushy-haired, mustachioed guy in a tux hollers, "I'm a fireman! Is anybody inside?"

Nobody thinks so, so the fireman starts hollering, "Everybody back! We'll need access!" and herding people out toward the parking lot.

"You have a car phone?" Dad shouts at him. "Has anybody called the firehouse?"

The fireman doesn't answer, just shouts, "Everybody back!"

Later on, the Vegas papers will call it a mob scene, but it isn't. There's no panic. It's no worse than the line for the Li'l Jeeter. Except for one guy in a business suit who's got a camcorder and is trying to buck the crowd to get in closer for better pictures, everybody's cool. Everybody behaves, everybody moves out of the courtyard calmly to clear the way for the fire trucks.

But the fire trucks aren't showing up. The firehouse is all the way at the other end of town. For all we know, they still might not have the news.

There's this incredible noise as part of the canopy collapses. As it dangles from metal cables, flames begin to lick at the main building. The fireman in the tux is arguing with the camcorder guy, pushing him back.

At last we hear sirens in the distance. I stand

198

on tiptoe and look toward Entertainment Way. It's bumper-to-bumper out there, and even though the sirens are getting louder, there's not even a glimmer of a flashing light heading in our direction. "Still must be a long way off."

"Stuck in traffic," Greb says morosely. "Figures."

"Second fire in three years," a voice says behind me. "Place is jinxed. Hoodooed."

I know that voice. I turn around. Zack waves his cigarette toward me. "Jinxed. Fact. Told you so."

Gilda and Wendy are crying. Makeup is streaming down their faces. "This is so terrible!" Gilda wails.

"I can't believe this!" Wendy shrieks. "I can't!"

"This is the worst thing that ever happened!" Gilda sobs.

"What's with her?" Caitlin asks me. "She took an instant course in sensitivity training?"

"Come on," says Greb. "She's just making a big public deal about this so everybody will *think* she's sensitive."

"I heard that, Dirk Greb!" Gilda shrieks. She winds up and kicks him in the butt.

"So much for sensitivity," I remark.

From out there in the parking lot, we can finally see the flashers on the fire trucks. Eventually they break free, head up the wrong side of Entertainment Way, and roll right past us into the courtyard. The firefighters are pretty impressive as they unroll the hoses and hook them up. I can see the fireman in the tux put on a raincoat, then help his mates set up the hoses.

"Well, they said the show wasn't over," Greb mutters.

"Beats some dumb old volcano for excitement," somebody says behind us.

And then a huge kid rips off his Volcanoes jacket. "Damn the volcano! Damn it!" he keeps shouting. He rips the Volcanoes lettering off the front of his jacket. He rips the cloth volcano off the back of his jacket. He tosses the jacket to the ground and stomps on it.

"I have the feeling we may be in for an official change of nickname," I say as the hoses are playing on the fire.

"The Pyromaniacs has a nice ring to it," says Caitlin.

"The Flames," says Greb.

"The Heat," says Caitlin.

We're giddy. Silly. Even Dad chimes in. "The Fire."

"The Blazes," I say.

"Hey, lay off," somebody behind us snaps. "There might be people still in there. Firefighters might still get hurt."

I do feel slightly guilty about making jokes, but making jokes is all I can do. "Hey, don't mind us," I say. "We're in the College of Comedy. We're just getting in practice for when school opens."

"Right," Greb adds. "Like in the year 3000."

NINETEEN

Greb has a point. From the time they get there, it takes the firemen nearly twenty minutes to get the fire out. That doesn't sound like much, but believe me, it's amazing just how much damage a fire can do in a hurry. When the flames have died down, the firemen keep pouring water on the building to make sure there isn't anything smoldering inside. So whatever's inside may not be smoldering, but it is definitely soggy.

"By now my permanent record is papier-mâché," I point out as we watch.

Greb shakes his head. "Best thing that could happen to mine."

"I'm heading back home," Dad announces. "Anybody want a ride?"

"We'll go back with Cait," I tell him. "Thanks, anyway."

"Not too late, huh?"

"Hey, this is our last non-school-night before school starts," I remind him.

"Don't bet on it." Dad heads for the car.

We watch the firemen awhile, but there's not much to see anymore. "This is depressing," Caitlin mumbles. She's right. We're bummed.

We go across to the Silver Bullet's Ten Gallon Coffee Shop to drown our sorrow in discount milkshakes. Some kids from Gaming sit down at the next table. They make joke bets on when the school will actually open. Or *if*.

Caitlin shakes her head. "The crazy thing is, if somebody had told me yesterday that the high school might burn down and I wouldn't have to start Sports for awhile, I would've shouted hooray. So why am I depressed now? Because this weird school may not be so bad after all? If it ever opens? Right?"

Right, but Greb and I are too bummed to answer. We just try to outgross each other with our straw noises as we slurp up the last of our shakes.

When we get back to the high school parking lot, most of the cars are gone. But the 5 Stars Gal is still up on her perch, shining brightly and revolving away like the proudest historical monument you've ever seen.

The firefighters are rolling up their hoses, putting their equipment on the truck. "How bad is it?" Greb hollers at one of them.

"Nobody got hurt," a woman hollers back from the top of a hook-and-ladder. "Hard to tell about the building till morning."

"What do you mean, hard to tell?"

"Some fire damage, a lot of water. They'll know better in daylight."

As we lurch up to our apartment building, we hear the news on the Finger City country radio station. Firefighters battled a raging inferno at the new Jeeter P. Carmody Regional High School. No injuries were reported, though the building sustained extensive damage. The opening of the school may be postponed, but there will be no official announcement until inspectors have a chance to evaluate the structure.

"Some night, huh?" Caitlin sighs as she lets us out.

"Unforgettable," I groan.

"Go Volcanoes," Greb says in a zipless tone as we go our separate ways.

It's about two-thirty in the morning. I'm wasted. Even the stars look dim. But Dad's still up, reading, when I come through the door. "Any news?" he asks.

"It's out. It's a mess. They're not saying how bad yet."

"That's a big complex," Dad says. "A lot of it'll probably still be fine. Provided they don't try to start up the volcano again."

"Yeah, but who wants to go to a school that's had two humongous fires in a couple of years? Maybe Zack's right. There's a jinx. Revenge of the ghosts."

"Bull. It's revenge of human error. People goofed. Those tarps shouldn't have been up there on the canopy. The volcano wasn't ready for prime time, either."

"Yeah. They gambled on it. And lost."

Dad shakes his head and takes a sip of beer. "That's what this town's all about. That's what this country's all about. Remember what I said about screwing up?"

"Kind of," I mutter.

"Well, you think anywhere else in the world people would try a cockamamy idea like this crazy high school of entertainment and hospitality and comedy in a hotel building with a fake volcano out front?"

"Maybe it'd be better not to try."

"Maybe. I have no idea whether they can make a go of this. But when you take a chance, sometimes things work out."

"Like the high school? Like your career as a classical musician?"

"I said 'Sometimes.' Not every time. Not even most of the time. You take educated risks. You take your chances. You don't always win. Hey, Ivan, a lot of what you do in life is what you take responsibility for. I've taught you that, right?"

I sigh. "Sure."

"Well, a lot of it is also luck. Things you can't do anything about."

"Like getting stuck moving here?"

"You got it."

"Or the high school catching on fire?"

"It's like that obnoxious gambling teacher keeps saying on those TV ads? 'You've got to play the cards that're dealt you?' Well, those are the cards you've got. You do the best you can with 'em."

"Kind of a lousy hand since we moved here," I mutter.

"Not so terrible," Dad says, pointing to my head. "You've got an ace of brains up there."

My ace of brains dreams about dancing fire-women who make Romeo and Juliet disappear. It is imagining what life would be like without high school, when the doorbell breaks in. I toss on a bathrobe and head for the door. It's a skinny, stringy-haired guy in a sombrero.

"Almost noon and still no announcement, man. Got to take matters in our own hands."

I rub the sleep out of my eyes, try to adjust to the sun streaming through the door. "What is that supposed to mean?" I ask groggily.

"Let's go down to the school and check things out."

I wash up, grab some juice, toss some clothes on. As we're waiting for the Carmody Car, Caitlin pulls up in the Incredible Hulk. "You heard any news?" I ask her as we get in.

"Same as last night. Still waiting for the official report from the inspectors."

We get stuck in traffic on Entertainment Way, but that's okay, because we can already see the school. The huge sign under the 5 Stars Gal is totally blank now, probably because nobody has any idea what happens next. Barriers that say POLICE LINE are everywhere. Behind the barriers, guys in hardhats are swarming all over the place.

"Look!" Caitlin points, but you don't exactly

need X-ray vision to see the damage. There's a big streak of black soot right up the front of the main building where the canopy used to be. There are holes and broken glass where there were windows yesterday.

"Pretty grim," Cait says as we turn into the Bullet lot.

"Not good," I agree.

The instant we get out of The Hulk, a smoke stench ten times worse than usual invades our nostrils and lungs and won't let go. "Pee-yew!" Greb says. "Pustuliferous!"

We make our way over to the school. "Should never have happened," says this guy in a dealer's outfit at the police barrier. "Never. There's definitely something wrong with the fire inspections in this town to let this happen twice. You ask me, they cut corners to get the job done too soon. Or maybe there was a bribe."

"Some people think it's jinxed," I mention.

The dealer takes a puff on his cigarette. "Some people see flying saucers."

Cait and Greb and I move along the barrier to get a better look. From what we can see, the only damaged part is the main building behind the volcano. The volcano itself looks fine, and so do the other four buildings. "Could be worse, I guess," Caitlin says.

"They might actually be able to fix a lot of this," I say.

We head back toward the front entrance, where all the action is. "The most suppurating damage had to be in the offices. And the casino," Greb says.

"I wonder if the fish tank survived," Caitlin says.

"Hey, look!" Greb shouts. He points to the sign under the 5 Stars Gal. A guy in a cherry picker is hanging huge letters on it.

THE SH is already up there. We stand and watch the rest: **O ... W ... G ... O ... E ... S ... O ... N**

THE SHOW GOES ON. All right! Caitlin gives me a big hug, and I hug back. Greb breaks in to give me a high five.

"Warty!" says Greb.

"Splendiferous!" I reply.

The guy hangs an exclamation point up there.

"That's Carmody," I say. "If it doesn't have an exclamation point, it's not official."

Greb runs over to the barrier and hollers at the guy in the cherry picker. "When, man? When?"

"Huh?" the guy hollers back over the noise of the machine.

"*When?*" Greb and I both shout at the top of our lungs. Caitlin joins us. "*WHEN?*"

The guy hangs a small **W** up there. "When?" he yells back.

"Yeah!" the three of us scream.

"Wednesday!"

"*Which* Wednesday?" Greb shouts.

"*This* Wednesday," the sign guy screams.

Caitlin squeals and squeezes my hand.

"GROOVE CITY!" Greb shouts, raising his fist in the air. "DREAD! BAD! FESTERING! WARTITIOUS!"

"Or something," says Caitlin, beaming at me.

TWENTY

School is a mess. The place just reeks of smoke. The air-conditioning doesn't work. The casino looks as though it was the set of a hurricane movie. The public address system just spits out distortion. About the only thing that looks half right is the fish tank, and it still doesn't have any fish.

Between all the confusion and the long lines for the elevators, everybody's late for everything. Our homeroom teacher, Ms. Wilgus, has just enough time to take the roll and hand out schedules. Which are all wrong.

"We know all about the schedule problems," she informs us. "We know. There were a bunch of last-minute computer glitches to be worked out. The fire interfered with the process."

"So what are we supposed to do?" somebody

asks. "I'm not even in the right College!"

"Just follow the schedules you've got," Wilgus says, "except remember to check the room assignment changes on the wall if any room number on your schedule has a second digit of one or three."

There's a loud groan from the class. The walls are plastered with complicated signs listing all the room changes on account of the fire. Just figuring out which building you're supposed to be in isn't easy even if you consult the map on the back of your class schedule.

"Groan away, gang. It'll all be straightened out in a day or two or a year or two." The bell rings. "Good luck!"

Greb and I run into each other as we step out of the elevators on the fifth floor of the Comedy wing. "Warts, man," Greb says as we head down the hall. "They've got me in two football classes and one basketball."

"I've got one Gaming session and a Hospitality. I guess that's why they don't have a computer science department."

We find our first-period class, Comedy 1. "Got any fire jokes?" Greb asks the teacher at the door. It's Logan, the wiry redheaded guy with the goatee who did the comedy routine at the preview.

"You hear about the fireman who quit because things were getting too hot for him?" he shoots back.

"This guy's fast," Greb tells me.

"And then there was the dalmatian who wanted to be a firedog, but his reputation was too spotty," the guy puts in before we can catch our breath.

"Fast," Greb says, but before he can finish, the teacher is already going, "And the guy who became a fireman because everybody told him to go to blazes."

Greb and I just mouth the word "fast," but we don't actually say it.

"Go. Take a seat," the guy says. "Don't take it far."

Most of the seats are already taken. The only ones left are in the front row.

The name on the blackboard is Joe "Killer" Logan. "Killer?" Greb mutters loud enough so everybody in the room can hear. "Gnarly!"

Logan whirls around like a short, wiry version of the devil. He points at Greb. "Cut my class. Find out how gnarly." He strokes his goatee and begins calling roll.

"Anders!"

"Here!"

I don't pay close attention. When you've got a name like mine, you're bound to be last, unless a Zytzface shows up. I'm busy looking around, trying to figure things out, wondering if the sprinklers in the ceiling actually have any water in them, wondering if any college will accept me on the basis of a great score in the Comedy Boards.

"Dunkel!"

"Present."

Oh, great. My cousin's in this class, too. Just my luck.

"Forget it, Dunkel," says Logan. "You won't get a better grade by giving me presents." Gilda's friends groan, but her enemies crack up.

"Greb!"

"Yo."

"Yo," Logan shoots back. "Which makes you the first yo-yo of the day."

I notice how weird the classroom is. It's obviously been slapped together from a couple of hotel rooms. True, there's a blackboard at the front, but there's also a wet bar at either end and a big mirror at the back. You half expect to see beds, but there aren't any.

"McKibbin!"

"Here."

Caitlin! I look back and she gives me this look as if to say she has no idea how she got here, but what the hey! All right!

"Pahinui!"

"Uh-huh."

Of course, there aren't any desks, either. We're sitting at folding tables on orange plastic chairs that have five stars on the backs. Those five stars repeat on the wallpaper. And the carpet, where there are almost as many stains as stars. If you look hard, you can figure out where the beds must have been.

"Zellner!"

I only half hear. I'm kind of dazed in the heat, I can already feel my underarms beginning to ooze, and I'm kind of hypnotized by the view out the window. Five stories down, girls are diving and watersliding into this enormous lagoon. If I use my imagination, I can almost make their clothes disappear.

"Anybody know an Ivan Zellner?"

Greb pokes me from the next table over.

"Here!" I say.

"Slow reaction, Zellner. Way too slow. The art of comedy is . . . . *timing!*" He slams his roll book on the desk so hard it makes me jump.

Logan half-sits on the corner of his desk. I suddenly notice the custard pies in the middle of it. "Okay! Up!"

I'm not sure if he means me or the entire class, but everybody else is still sitting down.

"Come on! Up! On your feet!"

"Me?" I squeak, pointing to myself.

"You?" The Killer sneers. "You? Let's not be hasty. Let's consider for a moment. Let's not jump to conclusions. Perhaps I was referring to the great Zellners of history. Where's Martha Washington Zellner? Elsie the Zellner Cow? Jo-Jo the Dogfaced Zellner?"

Giggles sneak out around the classroom.

"Late for class, apparently," says Logan. "You'll have to do."

I make a face and stand up slowly.

"Very good, Zellner. Now please come up front, and I do mean you, not Richard Nixon Zellner or Zellner the Hutt. Right here." He points to a spot in front of his desk.

I am beginning to understand how this guy got his nickname. I kind of shuffle to the front of the class.

Logan flashes the smile of an executioner. "Gentlemen and scabies, may I present Mr." — he checks the roll book for my first name — "*Ivan* Zellner."

I just stand there, confused. Logan repeats my name more theatrically, extending his hand toward me and the class as though he's introducing somebody on stage. "Mr. Ivan Zellner!"

I don't get it. I stand there some more.

Logan's smile turns wider and phonier. "Come on, Zellner. Ivan the Terrible. We're waiting. Be funny!"

Now I know what he means, sort of. I stall for time. "Be funny?"

Logan looks exasperated. "You in the wrong class, Zellner? Did you think this was Introduction to Undertaking?"

I can hear Gilda's thin, mean laugh over the rest of the class.

"Uh . . . no," I mutter.

"Well, what do you think it is?"

"Introduction to Comedy," I mumble.

"Can't hear you, Zellner. Speak up. Introduction to what?"

"Comedy," I say.

"Comedy! Then you are in the right class. And you're standing up. That makes you a stand-up comedian. So what are you waiting for? Come on. Make us laugh!"

I turn toward the class. A bunch of "show me" attitudes stare back. What now?

I mean, there is something scary about standing up in front of a roomful of people, some you know and lots you don't, and trying to figure out what might make them laugh, or at least smile, and realizing you probably are going to screw up royally and embarrass yourself.

When it comes to funny right this minute, my

mind is a total blank. I notice those custard pies, but Logan must be saving them for something. I glance around the room, hoping maybe I'll get an idea. Gilda is giggling and pointing at me. A couple of kids are sort of talking and gesturing to themselves; they probably figure their turn will come soon, so they're trying to practice.

Caitlin gives me this look that says she knows I can do it, but so far I can't. And worst of all is my great friend Dirk Greb, who's sitting there with a smirk that says something like "Come on, big fella, do your stuff."

Logan pokes my ribs with his pointing stick. "Come on, Zellner," he says. "Make a face. Tell a joke. Fall on your butt. Come on. We're ready. We're willing. We're able. We're waiting. Amuse us."

I scowl. I don't think making a face would make anybody laugh, and I'm not about to fall on my butt. Then I notice Gilda whispering to a friend of hers. I suddenly come up with the germ of an idea. A nasty idea, but an idea.

But before I can do anything about it, Logan cuts me off. "Okay, Zellner. I'll help you out." He begins writing on the blackboard.

When he finishes, he taps his pointer underneath what he's written. "Read it aloud, please."

"Rule Number One of comedy," I read. "Comedy is not easy."

"Agree or disagree, Zellner?"

"Agree," I mumble.

"Can't hear you, Zellner."

"Agree," I say louder.

"Thank you, Zellner."

I shrug and head back to my seat.

"Did I tell you to sit down, Mr. Zellner?" Logan asks without even turning toward me.

I stop in my tracks. "No," I mutter.

Logan's smile grows wider. He taps his pointer on the carpet in front of his desk. "Then please come back here and help me illustrate Rule Number Two."

I go back to the spot he's pointing to.

"Rule Number Two," says Logan, and I wait for what comes next. What comes next, from out of nowhere, is a custard pie right in the face.

The class howls. Gilda's tinny, nasty laugh rises high above the rest. That germ of an idea is getting bigger. It has something to do with noses. Big ones.

I can't see a thing, but a towel turns up in my hand. I wipe off the custard, which is actually shaving cream. And at that moment, a loud bell starts bonging. *BONG! BONG! BONG!*

"Okay, ladies and germs: Fire drill, or anyway, let's hope it's a drill. What is it they say in boxing, Zellner?"

I shrug. *BONG! BONG! BONG!*

Logan scowls. "Class?"

"Saved by the bell?" says Greb.

"Right," Logan replies. "Move it, gang, nice and orderly. Fire exit is down the hall to the left. No running. Do *not* use the elevators. Rule Number Two: Comedy is not impossible. And around here, as we know, neither is fire." *BONG! BONG! BONG!*

"Not terrible," says Logan as I hand back the towel. "You took that well for an amateur. Now, move it."

Caitlin flicks some shaving cream from my hair. "Hey, you were great!" *BONG! BONG! BONG!*

"Thanks," I reply, "even if it isn't true."

"True, man," says Greb. "Great. Grand. Warty, even."

"Come on, gang," Logan urges seriously. "Move it. We still don't know whether or not this is just another joke."

"Hey, we're not sure whether or not the universe is just another joke," says Greb. *BONG! BONG! BONG!*

"That's what you're here to find out," says Logan as we head down the fire stairs. "Just don't use this school as your sole source of evidence. Or Carmody, Nevada."

"Fast!" Greb and I say, giving each other high fives.

BONG! BONG! BONG!

TWENTY-ONE

The fire is a false alarm. Just a drill. Probably a good idea when you think about it.

But it gives me time to get my act together. "Saved by the bell" is right. On the way back, I even have time to swing by my locker. So when we get up to the classroom and Logan sticks me up front again with a big fanfare — I guess to illustrate Rule Number Three — hey, I'm ready!

I've got some gags. I've got some confidence. If all else fails, I've got those nose glasses from the Finger City Mall.

"Fires! Floods! Volcanoes!" I begin. "Let me put it another way: A funny thing happened to me on the way to high school . . ."

ABOUT THE AUTHOR

STEPHEN MANES has written more than thirty books for kids and adults, including *Chocolate-Covered Ants, The Great Gerbil Roundup, Some of the Adventures of Rhode Island Red,* and the Hooples and Oscar Noodleman series. Children in five states have voted his best-selling *Be a Perfect Person in Just Three Days!* their favorite book of the year. Its hero, Dr. K. Pinkerton Silverfish, recently returned in the sequel, *Make Four Million Dollars by Next Thursday!*

For more than ten years, Mr. Manes covered the computer industry for *PC Magazine, PC/Computing,* and *PC Sources.* He co-wrote the best-selling adult biography *Gates.*

Mr. Manes also writes screenplays, software, and place mats. He lives in Seattle, Washington.